SWITCHBLADE

switch·blade (swĭch′blād′) n.
a different slice of hardboiled fiction where the dreamers and the schemers, the dispossessed and the damned, and the hobos and the rebels tango at the edge of society.

THE JOOK
GARY PHILLIPS

I-5: A NOVEL OF CRIME, TRANSPORT, AND SEX
SUMMER BRENNER

PIKE
BENJAMIN WHITMER

THE CHIEU HOI SALOON
MICHAEL HARRIS

THE WRONG THING
BARRY GRAHAM

SEND MY LOVE AND A MOLOTOV COCKTAIL! STORIES OF CRIME, LOVE AND REBELLION
EDITED BY GARY PHILLIPS AND ANDREA GIBBONS

PRUDENCE COULDN'T SWIM
JAMES KILGORE

NEARLY NOWHERE
SUMMER BRENNER

OTHER WORKS
by Summer Brenner

FICTION

I-5, A Novel of Crime, Transport, and Sex
My Life in Clothes
The Missing Lover
One Minute Movies
Dancers and the Dance
The Soft Room

POETRY

From the Heart to the Center
Everyone Came Dressed as Water

NOVELS FOR YOUTH

Ivy, Homeless in San Francisco
Richmond Tales, Lost Secrets of the Iron Triangle

AUDIO

Arundo Salon, *Because the Spirit Moved*

ABOUT *NEARLY NOWHERE*

"With her beautifully wrought sentences and dialogue that bring characters alive, Summer Brenner weaves a gripping and dark tale of mysterious crime based in spiritually and naturally rich northern New Mexico and beyond."

—Roxanne Dunbar-Ortiz, historian and writer, author of *Roots of Resistance: A History of Land Tenure in New Mexico*

"Summer Brenner's *Nearly Nowhere* has the breathless momentum of the white-water river her characters must navigate en route from a isolated village in New Mexico to a neo-Nazi camp in Idaho. A flawed but loving single mother, a troubled teen girl, a good doctor with a secret, a murderous sociopath—this short novel packs enough into its pages to fight well above its weight class."

—Michael Harris, author of *The Chieu Hoi Saloon*

"To the party, Summer Brenner brings a poet's ear, a woman's awareness, and a soulful intent, and her attention has enriched every manner of literary endeavor graced by it."

—Jim Nisbet, author of *A Moment of Doubt* and *Snitch World*

"It's because the characters are so richly drawn, the writing so elegant, the rural western landscape so exquisitely described, that you don't realize at first what Brenner has done to you; how she's loaded up the dory, strapped you in, and loosed you down this terrifying river. And, then, of course, it's too late. *Nearly Nowhere* is a beautiful and chilling novel."

—Benjamin Whitmer, author of *Pike*

ABOUT *I-5, A NOVEL OF CRIME, TRANSPORT, AND SEX*

TOP TEN BOOKS OF 2009, Los Angeles Mystery Bookstore

TOP 50 BOOKS OF THE DECADE, BSC Review

"It has a quality very rare in literature: a subtle, dark humor that's only perceivable when one goes deep into the heart of this world's absurd tragedy, or tragic absurdity."

—R. Crumb

"This book bleeds truth—after you finish it, the blood will be on your hands."

—Barry Gifford, author of *Wild at Heart*

"Well-written, without a superfluous word, it's a big chase, practically a movie on the page."

—Ned Sublette, author of *Cuba and Its Music*, *The World That Made New Orleans*, and *The Year Before the Flood: A Story of New Orleans*

"Anya is a wonderful, believable heroine, her tragic tale told from the inside out, without a shred of sentimental pity, which makes it all the stronger."

—Denise Hamilton, author of *The Last Embrace* and editor of *Los Angeles Noir*

"I'm in awe. *I-5* moves so fast you can barely catch your breath. It's as tough as tires, as real and nasty as road rage, and best of all, it careens at breakneck speed over as many twists and turns as you'll find on The Grapevine. . . . [A] hardboiled standout."

—Julie Smith, author of Skip Langdon and Talba Wallis crime novel series and editor of *New Orleans Noir*

"[A] grim and gripping noir novel. . . . Brenner writes boldly and with seething clarity."

—Nina Sankovitch, author of *Tolstoy and the Purple Chair: My Year of Magical Reading*

"[A] hairy and perfect novel. . . . It does not hurt that Anya is the heroine to end all heroines. Brenner's book is an antidote for a wide range of complaints."

—magicmolly.tumblr.com

"[A] very smart and conscientious book. But that doesn't mean that it isn't also an immensely enjoyable book. Brenner is an elegant writer, with an ear for the kind of startling turn of phrase that catches the reader off-guard and reawakens them to the force of her story."

—Benjamin Whitmer, author of *Pike*

"A novel that will beat you up—chances are you deserve it. *I-5* cuts through layers of flesh to reveal the true heart of noir: that for every American dream there are a thousand nightmares. I have read no better novel in the genre. Roll over Willeford, tell Goodis the news."

—Owen Hill, author of *The Incredible Double* and *The Chandler Apartments*

"We learn Anya's story in layers, and we learn her character in actions that are never quite what we expect them to be. She kept me guessing all the way through this hallucinatory shadow-world tour."

—Jedidiah Ayre, *Ransom Notes: The BN Mystery Blog*

"Steeped in tension and biting black humor, this noir road-novel-cum-character-study is an impressive debut by a promising new voice."

—Garrett Kenyon, *Literary Kicks* blog

"Brenner did not set out to update *Ivan Denisovich* [by Aleksandr Solzhenitsyn], but the similarities are unmistakable. In both novels, the main characters are snatched from their families and delivered to remote places that function by a harsh new set of rules. . . . [B]oth characters also exhibit a sense of agency that helps them retain their humanity in brutish surroundings. . . . Amidst all the difficult questions, the lively depiction of villains and antiheroes in *I-5* make Brenner's novel a thrill to read."

—Matthew Hirsch, ZNet

"Having now read—and completely enjoyed *I-5*—I still think Summer Brenner is a poet, but one with notable narrative skills and a deep commitment both to her characters and to justice. . . . *I-5* is in this sense a political novel, though Brenner never lets this obstruct our view of her character. Anya is someone you will never forget."

—Ron Silliman, ronsilliman.blogspot.com

"Wholly original piece of dark fiction that never goes where you expect it to and ventures into uncharted waters. It's uncompromising in ways that should be exceptionally appealing to readers of dark fiction, *I-5* is as tough a crime tale as you're likely to find anywhere."

—BSC Review

"Summer Brenner provides an insider's look at the seedy world of sexual slavery. . . . Nothing gets sugar-coated, yet Brenner shows sincere sympathy and warmth for her characters. I found it hard to stop turning the pages."

—David Batstone, author of *Not for Sale*,
cofounder of Not for Sale campaign

"[A] journey marred with sex and crimes that exposes the harsh reality of the invisibility of women, immigrants, and the marginalized, struggling to survive."

—Opal Palmer Adisa, author of *Until Judgment Comes*, *Eros Muse*, *Caribbean Passion*, and *It Begins with Tears*

"Inspired by the events of 1999 in Berkeley when a 17-year-old Indian girl died of carbon monoxide poisoning. . . . Brenner took the incident many steps further, a tribute to her social conscience, especially her identification with immigrants and other marginalized groups, her feminism, and her considerable writing skills."

—Estelle Jelinek, *The Berkeley Daily Planet*

"Her prose style is a mirror reflection of the interstate: parched, fast, and tense, with an emotional timbre that matches the velocity of the plot."

—Rachel Swan, *East Bay Express*

NEARLY NOWHERE
SUMMER BRENNER
PMPRESS

Nearly Nowhere
By Summer Brenner

www.summerbrenner.com

A version of *Nearly Nowhere* was previously published in France as *Presque nulle part* by Gallimard's La Série noire, translation by Janine Herisson.

Quotes from *The Holy Bible*, Revised Standard Version, 1946.

A word of appreciation to Hannah Boal, Deb Dohm, Meredith LaVene, and Shael Love for their advice and expertise

Published by:
PM Press
PO Box23912
Oakland, CA 94623
www.pmpress.org

Cover illustration by Brian Bowes
www.brianbowesart.com
Interior design by Courtney Utt/briandesign

ISBN: 978-1-60486-306-2
Library of Congress Control Number: 2011939682
10 9 8 7 6 5 4 3 2 1

Printed in the USA on recycled paper by the Employee Owners of Thomson-Shore
in Dexter, Michigan.
www.thomsonshore.com

for Michael who took us there . . .

Presentiment—is that long Shadow—on the Lawn—
Indicative that Suns go down—

The Notice to the startled Grass
That Darkness—is about to pass—

—Emily Dickinson

PART I

I

From a hundred yards down the Zamora road in the back of a rusted wheelless and faded turquoise pick-up on the only way in and out of the village, Ruby Ryan lay shivering under a cotton blanket. Going to the fields, the Spanish farmers passed the human form in the truck. It was Ruby, Kate Ryan's teenage daughter. That, they knew. Accustomed as they were to the shape and stupor of alcohol and drugs in their own families, they paid little attention. They climbed the paths behind the gas station to the precipitous arid plots of land where they surveyed their rows of green chile and squash, the trickling water in the irrigation ditches. They crossed themselves.

"With water life is not bad," they concurred. Then, crossed themselves again.

They believed they were fortunate it was Taos, not Zamora, that artists, anthropologists, tourists, and Texans discovered decades ago. Zamora had remained poor and shabby, an inhospitable village on a serpentine back road. Neither quaint nor friendly, it had a reputation as a place travelers should pass through quickly. Nothing *típico* of New Mexican charm had been put on display. No strings of red chiles on the doors. Or terra cotta pots of flowers under whitewashed porticos. Or hand-painted signs to the old church or ruin, the glassblower or weaver.

Only once in recent memory had an intruder violated the village's unspoken rule and erected a road stand for his raku pots. Sales were not only nil but the village storekeeper refused his business. A month later, his trailer was burned and he fled.

Afterwards, ominous stories about Zamora spread to other members of the nomadic white tribe looking to attach themselves to authentic identities and cheap land. Zamora was authentic and the price of dry earth cheap, but the atmosphere was hostile and tough. Only gringos with something to hide took delight in its dilapidated houses and rusty junk.

Ruby lay on a piece of smelly foam, her head on her denim jacket. Tossed around the truck were her cowboy boots, socks, a dingy brassiere, a few empty cans of Coors. Since her mom's new boyfriend arrived, Ruby spent more nights in the truck than at home.

2

"Well, how about it?" Troy growled, his look suggesting Kate was welcome to make his coffee.

Kate ignored him. For two days, her opinion of Troy Mason had concentrated solely on his departure. When he charmed his way home with her from a bar in Española, he needed a place for one night. So far, he'd hung on for four weeks.

He growled again.

"I don't think so," Kate replied, her eye glancing at his naked body that now bored her to contempt.

He stretched and scratched himself like a happy pet. He guessed he'd have to get his own coffee.

"Did you try the pick-up?" he asked, trying to fake an interest in Kate's pain-in-the-ass daughter.

"I didn't get that far down the road."

"She's probably there with August."

"Probably," Kate said.

"What you got going today?" he asked, ever familiar and easygoing. He seemed to have all the time in the world.

"Besides kicking your ass out?" she winked.

"I still got the rings to finish." His own wink slow and suggestive as if everything about a car suggested a woman's body.

Kate had to admit mechanics were the centerpiece of her sporadic romantic life. In the mountains, they vied with underground chemists as the most important of the practical arts.

"There's a mess in here to clean up." Kate's gaze swept the room past the hanging bed, wood stove, sink. Everything needed dusting. Always. The rugs needed beating. A load of wash waited to be run and line-dried before the rain. Another pile, board stiff from sun, needed folding. Her work table, a solid door on two sawhorses, was in disarray.

Kate's work wasn't dependable or lucrative. The best you could say about growing medicinal plants was the satisfaction it brought her. Although the mainstay of her scanty livelihood, gas to Santa Fe and

Albuquerque and a bite of lunch too often devoured any profits. If the car broke down, it put her in debt for months. In the fall, she would have to reconsider other options.

"I got stuff to run to Old Town," she said.

Troy was amused. In general, women amused him, especially those with modest schemes for success.

"What stuff?" he indulged her. He found women quaint.

"Sage, borage, mint, black cohosh, broom, it's the car holding things up."

"It'll be finished this morning. You want things done right?"

"Shit," she sighed.

"You know what's holding me up, baby? It's something bigger than an engine." Troy's cloying complaint. "With what I'm waiting on, you can buy twenty cars."

Kate's lips twisted. Having to listen to Troy's bullshit was part of the penance of having listened to it in the first place on a starry night at Shorty Stack's Bar and Grill, aided and abetted by a few margaritas. She'd believed him. It was the same bright-eyed hopefulness that endeared her to the farmers of Zamora. She believed.

The drifters who appeared from time to time in Kate's life wanted to fix her car, chop her cords of wood, build a shelf or shed, work in the garden. It was barter economy. Her end was shelter, food, sex. For a brief while, it was a pleasure to have reminders of adult male company. Occasionally, the man confessed to love her, hoping for an indispensable place in her domestic life. Within weeks, Kate had tired of the arrangement. "Intrusion," she called it. "Invasion" if it got bad.

Without qualms, Kate asked them to leave. Sometimes, there was a feeble protest but rarely trouble. After all looming in her backyard were the vestiges of Coronado's royal loyal army. If it was a question of logistics, she gave them a ride out of Zamora to Santa Fe and loan of a few dollars. Loan was a misnomer. None of them ever paid her back.

3

Ruby drowsed in the back of the truck, wishing she could plunge into a body of water. A warm gulf, vast ocean, becalmed sea, river. Specifically the Salmon River, where her aunt had a house. Her happiest memories were on the river.

But Ruby's fate was landlocked. Dry dusty ground, scrubby plants, monotonous blue skies, and panoramic vistas of the same shit in all directions. A desert prison, emblematic of thirst, filled with brown barren mountains, brown dirt fields, brown adobe houses.

"Water," she smacked her lips. A reminder it was time to go home. She zipped her jeans, stuffed her bra in a back pocket, grabbed her boots, and headed down the dusty road.

"Hey, you!" Kate called from the garden.

Ruby sauntered across the yard, her breasts high and firm on her statuesque torso. Her sturdy curvaceous rump swinging side to side. At sixteen, she was four inches taller than her mother and outweighed her by twenty pounds. She wasn't as dark as other hippy kids who weren't all gringo. They were regarded as Hispanic, Latino, Indian, Native, but not Ruby. *Mulatto* used to be the word but no one said that anymore.

"Where you been, Ruby Ryan?" Kate's voice trilled. As usual, she was trying too hard.

Ruby hated when her mother made their encounters seem like normal happy events. Kate's cheerfulness in the ruins of their existence was an insult to common sense.

"In my penthouse, *n'est-ce pas*?" Ruby sneered, ambling to her mother's side and planting a desultory kiss on her cheek. A loveless gesture that passed as affection in Kate's mind.

"How about breakfast?" Kate cooed. She was coddling but she'd be delighted to make *huevos rancheros* with tortillas, homemade green chile, fresh-squeezed juice for her girl.

"I'd puke," Ruby said.

Kate swallowed her words. A critique would run Ruby into her room or back to the truck. Instead, she turned to the mountains and sky. Zamora was a place for gods if there were gods.

"Been drinking?" Kate couldn't resist.

Sucking the ends of her hair, Ruby stumbled around the chickens and flats of seedlings, entered the door, and slouched to her room, avoiding the toxic dump site called Troy Mason.

4

"Your little girl don't like me much," Troy said.

"She doesn't like anything," Kate said.

"She'd like me if I had money to throw around." He rolled from underneath Kate's Dodge Power Wagon and shaded his eyes from the sun.

"Ruby doesn't give a damn about money," Kate retorted.

Troy whistled. "Spoiled all the same," he said, taking his time like a windup pitcher. "You got a piece of top-grade filet mignon you left out the fridge. You left it so long it turned gray and stinky. Spoiled so bad, it rotted." In his opinion, spoiled from the get-go by a nigger dad.

"Shut up, Troy!" Kate said.

"Spoiled don't mean what people think. People think you give too much to a kid like toys and shit, it spoils them. That ain't what happens. What happens is the kid don't get taken care of like put in the fridge until it's time to eat. It don't get disciplined or told right from wrong. That's spoiled. What's sad is the kid was born okay." He paused to make his consummate point. "But the parents went and spoiled it."

Kate walked to the cottonwood. It was almost cool under the parasol of leaves.

"Time to go, Troy," she said decisively.

"Spoiled is when people believe they *owed*. Like deserve to go to heaven because they believe in God. You know what I think? I don't think anybody is owed nothing."

"Meaning everyone is owed something," Kate laughed nastily. "Or no one is owed anything."

"You acting prissy?" Troy skipped a lug wrench across the ground. "Cause it don't take a real high IQ to live in a dirt house, Kate. You live up here doing nothing and think somebody owes you for doing such a good job. You left your fancy family, your fancy college, and slummed it up. You fucked some rednecks and niggers."

Kate flinched.

"You had a little bastard girl and bought a piece of dirt in a dirty dirt town in the middle of goddamn nowhere. But like everybody else, you ain't owed a goddamn thing. Everything I got I had to work for it."

"What you got?"

"You talking to me?" he spat.

"I asked what you got."

"I got my condo on Maui. I got my silver Porsche 550 Spyder, same year as James Dean. I got a mahogany sailboat in San Francisco, sleeps eight. I got beautiful kids, you seen them. I got it all, but I'm just hard up right now. I ain't been on this side of the fence since the war."

"I heard," she said.

Halfway up the mountain from Shorty's, Kate stopped believing Troy after he took out his wrinkled photos of cars, houses, yachts, a few blond kids and smoothed them on her dashboard.

"You doubting me?" he asked.

There was no answer. Out of confusion, guilt, cowardice, compassion, Kate didn't want to confront the man with the fact he was a liar. Maybe born that way, maybe not.

Ruby emerged from the house.

"Hey!" she said.

It was the friendliest sign Kate had had in days.

Ruby wanted a ride to town. She wanted to go swimming.

"Car ain't ready," Troy said, pleased to disappoint her.

Ruby stared at him. She hated Troy more than anything.

"Not doubting but you still have to go," Kate said.

"After Iraq I wanted to get to Libya, Syria, Egypt, all those rag-head places." Troy's voice swelled.

"And what?" Ruby sniggered. "They wouldn't send you?"

"By the time your daddy made it there, they were fucking desperate."

Ruby jumped on Troy's back. She hooked her arm around his throat and squeezed his ribs with her thighs. "You piece of white ignorant scum!"

"Get off before he kills you!" Kate yelled.

Troy cursed and bucked Ruby to the ground, spun around, and planted his foot on her throat. Kate lifted the shovel and charged. The shovel he seized and threw across the yard. Then, twisting both women's arms, he marched them into the house, one small and sprightly like an Arabian, the other unbroken and brown.

Across the road, the Spanish farmers watched the fight. They knew Kate Ryan was a woman who kept to herself when a man was around. They appreciated that. They also knew she wasn't a drunk or a crazy. Their wives liked her homemade jams and homemade bread. Almost daily, they recalled she stanched an artery at the scene of an accident and saved one of their own. They knew her daughter to be out of control like their own teenagers. Uniformly, they did not trust the newcomer, Troy.

"We're making a few rules here and now!" Troy raised his fist and banged it on the wall.

"Like *your* rules?" Ruby's eyes rolled.

"Shut up!" he roared.

"My house! My rules!" Kate declared.

"Shut up!"

Kate tried to move, but Troy grabbed her neck and threw her into a chair.

"I ain't saying you can leave," he said.

"He's crazy," Ruby whispered.

"No telling what I'll do," Troy snarled.

"What do you want?" Kate asked coolly.

Ruby had never seen her mother so cool.

"Take me to the bank. That's what I want."

"Don't give him our money, Mom! Please don't give it to him!"

Troy swatted Ruby's cheek, leaving a trickle of blood.

"Don't you dare touch her!" Kate lunged for Troy's wrist. "Or I'll call the sheriff!"

A laugh rushed from the pit of his abdomen as he ripped the phone from the wall. "Call him, Kate. Tell him I hit your little girl. And then," Troy doubled over, "tell him I'm taking money you got growing plants with your bare hands."

5

The farmers of Zamora were not Mexican, Hispanic, Chicano, or Latino. They were Spanish. They traced their ancestry directly to the latifundia grants awarded by the King of Spain to Coronado's men for their explorations and conquests as they ventured north from the Sonoran desert toward El Dorado, trudging over a thousand miles, invading and disrupting the peaceful sedentary farm life of the Pueblo Indians.

Two hundred years after the soldiers were granted huge tracts of land, it was appropriated by gringo ranchers and thieves, leaving most of the Spanish dynasties destitute. Generations had farmed in the Sangre de Cristo mountains since their ancestors chased gold through the New World. As it turned out, gold was the place itself. The poor soil that had to be nourished, the limited water that had to be conserved, the common bonds of hardship.

For the second time that year, Hector Trujillo entered Kate Ryan's yard. The first was to shoot a large white rooster that chased Kate to the shed where she'd flung herself on the roof, waiting for the bird to wear himself out. Kate gave him the carcass to take home for green chile stew.

That was May after a late snow. A week of omens and incidents. Hector's daughter ran off to Las Vegas. His water pipes burst. His youngest brother slipped on the frozen ground and cracked his head.

When Hector entered Kate Ryan's yard this time, he knew he was trespassing into a private matter. A lover's quarrel, no business of his. It would cost him. It would likely bring trouble on his head. Everything led to trouble, he knew.

Nevertheless, he told himself, "A son-of-a-bitch is a son-of-a-bitch." The simple truism gave him courage to walk across the yard to Kate's window.

Through the glass, he spotted Kate's daughter, Ruby. He never failed to notice how devilishly pretty she was, the color of cocoa like his daughter, a color heightened by unruly red-streaked hair, green eyes, and an insolent vaginal-colored mouth. There was fresh blood on her cheek.

Troy stood in profile, calm and composed. Hector recognized his calm. It was the satisfaction of a man whose demands have been granted through superior physical strength. He had the same look whenever he beat his kids.

Kate Ryan was not in sight. Whether she was hurt or unconscious, he couldn't be sure. Noiselessly, he backed away from the house and crossed the yard to the road. When he reached the edge of the field, he began to trot. Dust and globes of dry sagebrush scattered by the wayside.

"Hector, I ain't seen you run in a hundred years," Marcos shouted as village dogs started to bark.

"Kate Ryan," Hector said breathlessly. "Get your gun."

Marcos was younger and thinner. He could sprint. The sight of two men running, whose habit of slow pace was known as key to a long healthy life, sent an alarm through the village.

"What's wrong, Marcos?" a neighbor called.

"Tell me, man!"

The brothers were too excited to speak. At the entrance to his adobe house, Hector collapsed into his wife's arms with Marcos right behind him. By this time, the Martinez twins and Juan Pedro had joined them.

"Hector says Kate Ryan killed."

Hector nodded in a way that neither denied nor confirmed.

"The girl taken hostage."

Hector nodded but the meaning was unclear.

The men of the newly formed posse looked into each other's eyes, eyes that were brown, weathered, aroused. Their expressions were confident with purpose. As proud descendants of the first conquerors of the New World, they would exact justice.

"Call the sheriff," Hector's wife pleaded. "We have the telephone."

"Too far" was the consensus.

"I will call the sheriff," Marie Luisa announced. "After you kill this man you say killed Kate Ryan, the sheriff will come and arrest you! They will take you away to prison. Hector! Your own children will starve!" she screamed, pulling her husband's hair and pounding his chest.

Hector's oiled cleaned loaded 22-gauge shotgun was mounted behind the wooden door. Marcos had a gun too. The Martinez twins and Juan Pedro retrieved hoe, sickle, and scythe from the tool shack by the corner of the house.

The women did not bless or smile on the little band. Instead, they prayed for lightning to spark a fire in the field. Or flip a truck on the road. Or crash a plane into the mountainside. They prayed for a miracle to stop Hector, Marcos, the Martinez twins, and Juan Pedro from entering Kate Ryan's yard.

Their prayers went unanswered.

The men marched on with a pack of dogs yapping after them.

At the entrance to the Ryan property, Hector shouted, "Hey! Hey! Kate Ryan!"

The hollow sound was carried away by the rising afternoon wind.

Troy didn't hear the shout, but he appeared at the door. Astonished at the sight of an assembly of armed men, he ducked into the house and scrambled for anything that could serve as a weapon.

Kate was readying herself for the drive down the mountain. She splashed her face and armpits with water. She changed into a skirt and embroidered Oaxacan blouse. She took off her work boots and put on strappy sandals. She clasped a beaded necklace around her neck and braided her hair. She looked fresh and pretty.

"What got you?" she asked with alarm.

"Out there!" Troy pointed to the window. He'd plucked a chainsaw from the corner and was trying to pull the choke.

"Put it down before you hurt yourself," Kate commanded.

Troy obeyed. He lay the chainsaw on the floor and replaced it with a broom.

Ruby chuckled under her breath. She'd been scared, but at the sight of Troy with a broom, she convulsed with laughter.

Kate peered out the window at Hector and Marcos Trujillo and their cousins. She counted two guns and several farm implements.

"What'd you do?" she turned viciously to Troy.

Troy shook his head. If he could avoid it, he never mixed with Mexicans. Growing up, he'd seen them praying to pictures, fingering beads, burning incense, eating little wafers of flesh. Coronado, Cortez, all of them were curses on the earth. Whatever Kate believed about their royal ancestry, impoverished dignity, injustices suffered from ranchers and gringo law, nothing penetrated Troy's Texas prejudice.

"Did you do something?" Kate wheeled toward Ruby.

"That's Juan Pedro," she stammered.

"So it is." Kate stared past Ruby's shoulder. "Does he have a reason to kill us?"

A couple of weeks ago, Juan Pedro had frightened Ruby. He came to the truck where she sometimes slept. He stood only inches from her with a simple request. He wanted to *smell* her hair.

"I guess he likes me," Ruby said.

"And?"

"I told him to go fuck himself," Ruby was pleased to report.

6

As soon as Hector saw Kate Ryan, he threw down his gun. He ran and flung his arms around her. "We thought you were dead!" he shrilled.

"He saw the slash on your daughter's cheek," Marcos, the Trujillo brother with greater powers of reason, explained. "He jumped to conclusions." Marcos tipped his Isotopes baseball cap. "When he jumps, we follow."

"It's nothing," Ruby said, touching her cheek where Troy's ring nicked her.

"My eldest brother, he worries for your safety living usually alone and by yourself in the mountains with only Jesús and us to protect you."

Kate smiled at her circle of neighbors.

What Marcos omitted was no one ever worried when Kate was alone. The only cause to worry was when she took in a man like a stray dog. Stray dogs, as everyone knew, were legal to shoot.

"What my baby brother says is true," Hector uttered solemnly.

"Thank you, thank you all," Kate said with studied formality. Formality was the mutual framework they acknowledged. "For your protection and good will. My daughter has had a slight accident, and our friend?" Kate gestured to the door where Troy had taken a defiant stance. "He is leaving momentarily for California."

Hector and the others crossed the road. They were proud disaster had been averted in Zamora. And relieved to learn whatever privileges Kate Ryan had granted her recent guest would soon be ended.

Kate turned to Troy. "I saved your ass."

His eyes admitted it was true.

"You got your things?" she asked.

Troy shuffled his feet. He looked despondently at his Army duffle crammed with worn-out clothes, a sleeping bag, a manila envelope of random photographs of home interiors, expensive cars, other people's children, a sailboat called *Jaguar* nestled in a sparkling bay. He dreaded having to hit the road, forced to take any ride that stopped, finding his way to his sister's dump in San Diego. He dreaded having to resume the hunt for a weak link, someone vulnerable where he could play his tired hand.

He found life very pleasant in the Blood of Christ mountains. He liked the sweet fresh air and light that outlined the world like a vision from the Bible. It was pleasant lying next to a pretty lady who mostly minded her own business. He wished he could make it up to Kate Ryan. He snuck a glance at her painted toes sticking out of her sandals.

"Our money," Ruby protested.

"After I drop him off, we can get ice cream and go to the movies." Kate started forward toward Ruby. "Come on," she said.

"No," Ruby mumbled, clamping the headphones over her ears. *Fuck you!* the music said. Ruby echoed its sentiments.

7

ugust was stoned. He sniffed his way across the garden, ambling into patches of roses, squash, and melon. By the time he reached the back of the house, he felt as if he'd been wandering for hours. The black velveteen curtain over Ruby's window had fallen to the side. Through the glass, he watched her. Her head locked inside her earphones, her legs sprawled.

"Ruby!" he tapped.

She looked up. "What are you doing, asshole?"

"Nothing," he raised his hands guiltily.

"Why are you out there?" She pointed for him to come through the front door.

"I didn't want to disturb your mom and Troy," he said.

"Disturb?" Ruby made a face from the plague.

"I guess so," August gagged on laughter.

"Guess so?" she asked, wishing he'd go away.

"Like disturb," he said, losing the thread of conversation.

"Did you bring something?"

August removed a slender joint of *sensamilla*, the best weed in the Rio Grande valley, grown by his Uncle Gilbert. Ruby struck a match to its tip, and the rich narcotic smell rushed into her nostrils.

"Listen," she said, turning up the volume of a trumpet solo. The music was high and cool. The weed made it jump into the ozone.

"Miles," she said with awe.

"As in miles and miles?"

"As in Davis, asshole."

August pulled at the hairs of his ponytail. Ruby always knew what was cool which was why he worshipped her. She blew off school and knew everything while he toiled like a troll.

"Quinn sent it," Ruby said.

August sucked on the joint. He didn't want to share Ruby with Quinn or Miles or anybody. They smoked in silence, listening. Everything slowed down. One trumpet note took seconds to find the next.

"Is everything cool?" he asked.

"Most cool," she said.

"How come?"

"My mother's turd left today."

August eyebrows fluttered. "I was thinking of your mom, digging on that scumbag."

"And it freaked you out?"

August couldn't admit it excited him.

"It freaked you out, didn't it?"

"Miles what?" he asked.

"Miles Cool."

"Can we listen to music that doesn't fuck with my head?"

"Like?"

"Like the Beatles?"

Ruby laughed viciously. August's triteness permeated everything.

"Let's knock for it. Rock!" she said.

"Paper covers rock," August slapped his hand over hers. A thrill stirred his loins.

"Bullshit!" Ruby yanked her hand away. "Rock smashes paper! Rock smashes scissors! Rock smashes rock and makes sand! Rock rules!"

8

The thunderheads of summer afternoons in the high desert rose in the west. Black turrets spilling over deep blue, rolling across mesas, mountains, pueblos, villages, towns. A hundred miles away, a portcullis of rain fell onto the mesas. The water swelling the arroyos from dry riverbeds to dangerous currents, all the while moving steadily east. By sunset Zamora would be drenched.

Kate and Troy traveled slowly down the mountain.

"Runs good," he said, listening to the downshift from third to second. He was raised fixing things. Whenever he got into a pinch, he took a job at a garage. "Runs good," he repeated with pride.

"Like a top," she murmured.

In New Mexico, a reliable mechanic was more valuable than a lover. In fact, Troy wasn't much of a lover but he was an ace with cars. When they made love, she tried prompting him to relax but his mind was too busy. Most men's minds were too busy.

"Where will you go?" Kate tried to sound empathetic.

Troy rested his arm along the back of the seat, regarding Kate's pretty profile, pretty blouse.

"Maybe you'll fly over to Maui." He passed her a sly smile. "Ever been to Maui?"

"No," she said. In photos, Hawaii looked like suburbia in the tropics.

"We can hike into the center of Hanna-Akala. It's emerald inside the crater. Emerald," he sighed poetically.

New Mexico was the antithesis of emerald. Later when the rains came, the browns would darken into purple, magenta, prune, mud. In the valleys the cottonwoods, apple trees, chile fields would drink the rain. In town lawns and flower beds would drink the rain. But as soon as the rain swept over and was gone, everything would look thirsty and dry again.

"We'll stay at my condo," he snapped his fingers. "I got a bamboo bar by a picture window with a view of the Pacific. A swimming pool with a thatched cabana. You'd like it, Kate, I promise."

Kate's eyes fixed on the road, counting the miles and minutes into town. Whether Troy was flimflam, quack, victim, or crook, he was tiresome. However, her parentage dictated a fascination with such men. Her father had been convicted of embezzlement. For twenty years he'd stolen money to purchase their large home, large cars, luxury family vacations. Maybe he was smarter or luckier than Troy. A thief instead of a fantasizer. She and her father weren't in touch. She'd only seen him twice since he got out prison.

Troy caressed her hand. "I'm sailing the *Jaguar* to Hawaii in October. Maybe you'll come along."

9

ugust removed his shirt, hoping Ruby might notice his tight little muscles. He'd been lifting weights. Alas, Ruby never noticed anything about him. She only let him fool around if she was drunk. Then, she might agree to hump him in the truck. A Pyrrhic victory for August for while his lust was sated, his pride was demolished.

He put his shirt back on. His left foot was asleep. His jaw ached.

Ruby conceded he could play the Beatles. "But only *Rubber Soul*," she said.

"Want to smoke another joint?" he asked, falling back on the pillow.

"Got some?"

"I thought you did."

"Maybe Troysaurus Rex left his stash."

"Would he do that?"

"He was in a hurry," Ruby snickered. "When Hector and *familia* showed up with guns, the dude thought a mob had come to string him up. It was scary."

"Feel this," August said, curling her fingers around his biceps.

"Righteous, dude."

"It's good, isn't it?"

"Good? What's good about it?"

August's brain shrank. It always came to this. She made him feel stupid. He hated her. Then, he decided he was stupid and respected her honesty.

"Find the pot," he said dejectedly.

Ruby swung her knobby feet off the bed and placed them on the rug. Staring down, she listened to the sweet familiarity of the Beatles. Their voices suggested life was sweet. She could once remember feeling as light as their music.

"What are you doing?" he asked impatiently.

"Looking at the rug," she said.

Beneath her was an antique Navajo rug, its asymmetrical design woven in black, beige, and red bars.

"Haven't you looked at it a million times?"

"I like looking at it."

"Are you stoned?" he asked.

"I like looking at things, asshole. Like I don't have to be stoned to like it. Especially things people make. Somebody *made* this rug. Somebody I never saw and will never see because she's dead. I look at this rug every day. It tells me something deep."

"Ru-by," August stuttered with amazement. He loved listening to her. It turned out smart girls were sexy. No one was as smart and sexy as Ruby Ryan.

"Red dye used to come from crushed bugs, millions of scaly cactus bugs. Somebody hand-dyed the wool in the rug."

August wasn't really interested in dyes. He wanted Ruby to be impressed with his muscles.

"Go find the pot," he said.

Ruby stumbled around the house, rummaging in cupboards and on shelves, scanning the *vigas*, checking behind the fridge and under the sink. She located a baggy in her mother's treadle sewing machine. A baggy marked HM with a pink Sharpie. She sniffed. It was pot. She filled a soapstone pipe, lit a match, sucked on the stem. A single deep inhalation followed by a crash.

"Ruby," August called out.

Ruby lay on the rug next to Kate's bed, a larger rug with different colors and a different design. August contemplated that it was made by somebody, a Navajo long dead, a woman whose great-great-grandmother learned her craft from the Spaniards and taught it to her daughters and granddaughters, whose husbands and sons raised sheep and who dyed the wool with cochineal to make it red.

10

Kate withdrew $380 from her savings account. A debt of sorts or at least, payment for repairs on the car. A few hundred dollars bought his absence and atoned for her mistake. Kate thought money felt most valuable when it was worth something to someone else.

"Want a beer?" he asked, trying to hold on.

"I'll give you a lift to the bus station," she said. At least, she should get the satisfaction of watching him ride away.

"I got to see my lawyer first. But if the money is still held up, I'll hitch. It's a straight shot on 40."

"You got bus fare in your hand."

"I guess I'll get a beer." His blue eyes glittering as if that were all the future a man needed.

Kate extended her hand to shake. Business transpired, business complete. "Good luck," she said, although "good riddance" was what she meant.

Troy waved *adios* and headed from the Plaza to Jackson's Bar.

Halfway up the mountain, the sky burst. Over the surface of slick road, Kate drove by faith, sending prayers to Saint Christopher for safe travel, Buddha for detachment, and Mary Magdalene for Ruby's well-being. Instead of one hour, it took almost two to get home as sheets of rain pounded dust to mud.

By the time she reached Zamora, the storm had moved east. The village was silent, the road empty, the birds and insects mute, the dogs sleeping, the chickens quiet, the air cool and pristine. Not a bark, cluck, caw, or motor disturbed the peace.

When Kate entered her front door, peace vanished.

"What the hell!" she shouted, dropping to Ruby on the floor.

Ruby's hands were cold, her face ash. Kate felt for her pulse. She rubbed her temples and wrists. She pulled a quilt from the bed and tucked it around her.

"Ruby, Ruby, Ruby Ryan," she whispered urgently.

A few feet away, August stood frozen, his hands outstretched like a preacher, humming a Beatles song.

"Dope?" Kate hissed.

He nodded.

"Yours?"

August pointed to a baggy across the room.

"Run to the clinic! Get the doctor!" she commanded.

"We weren't doing anything."

"Find Dr. Tanner."

August put on his sandals and jumped out the door. Kate heard his feet, thwacking through the puddles in the muddy yard.

"Run, August, run," she said.

11

The county clinic, located a quarter-mile south on Highway 76, was a cinder-block building wedged between a house and abandoned garage. David Tanner kept regular office hours on weekdays, mostly caring for native villagers and their families. His nurse, Elaine Beasley, rented an adobe behind the clinic. She was available on weekends and evenings to contact the doctor in case of emergency.

"*Buenas tardes*," Elaine said to August.

"Hey," he mumbled, trying to hold his eyes open.

In the mountains Elaine saw many strung-out youth. She kept tabs on their missteps. In her opinion, August wore the mark of a boy who would turn out well. However, today he looked quite agitated. His eyes were half-closed, his face and ponytail wet with perspiration, his feet brown to the ankles with mud.

"Is Dr. Tanner here?" he panted.

"Anything wrong?" Elaine solicited.

"I need to see Dr. Tanner A-SAP."

"Okay, but he's with a patient right now. Is there a problem I can help with?"

"It's personal," August shivered. He was cold and hot.

"He'll be finished in a minute."

It was long uncomfortable minute.

Finally, Dr. Tanner emerged with Marie Luisa Trujillo, Hector's wife. Mrs. Trujillo smiled at August. David extended his hand in a strong shake, man to man. He met August when he first arrived in New Mexico. In fact, he once invited August's mother on a date.

"Can I speak to you alone?" August asked.

Dr. Tanner led the way into his private office. He pointed to a chair. He leaned against his large roll-top desk.

August's tongue was heavy, inert. He couldn't make it operate.

"You wanted to speak to me?" David prompted.

"Yes," August said, hugging his arms across his chest and searching for the right words. There were right words, but he couldn't find them. "Ruby Ryan," he muttered.

"Is Ruby ill?" Tanner pressed.

Those were the words.

"Really ill," August said.

12

Within minutes, the mandragora tea took effect and Ruby vomited into her mother's lap.

"Better," Kate said and burst into tears.

After another few minutes David Tanner appeared with August. In one stride, he dropped to Ruby's side, checked her pulse, her temperature, and ordered August to fetch water and towels.

"Good sign," he said, looking at Kate's lap.

It appeared the crisis had passed. Ruby was not going to die of an overdose. At least, not today.

"Is this the culprit?" David raised the pipe. He took a whiff of the ash. He licked the inside of the baggy. Weed and smack.

"Whose is this?" he asked.

"I don't know," Kate said.

"Where'd you get this?" he asked.

"It was my fault," August tried to say.

"Mom's sewing machine," Ruby said listlessly.

"You did not," Kate protested.

"He left it."

"Don't lie." Kate blushed with shame.

"Who left it?" David asked, his glasses pushed up his forehead.

"Troy," Ruby said.

"Who's Troy?"

No one answered.

"Is Troy your friend?" David turned to Ruby.

"God no! He's a fucking scumbag!" she sputtered.

"Who is Troy?" David repeated. "Would someone tell me?"

"A friend of mine," Kate offered weakly.

"A junkie?"

"I don't think so," Kate said.

"Car mechanic?"

Kate nodded.

David recalled a handsome cowboy specimen he'd seen at the

market. Taller and slimmer than David with a lot more hair, he remembered the bright blue jittery eyes. He'd heard he was good with cars. David traced the pink letters HM on the baggy.

"Is there more?" he asked.

"I don't think so," Ruby said.

Kate searched the Singer's compartmentalized drawers designed for bobbins, spools, needles, pins.

"Not here," she reported.

"Is there more?" he turned harshly to Ruby.

"How would I know? Ask Troy," she pouted.

"Can we ask him now?" David insisted.

"I just drove him to Santa Fe."

"Does he live here?"

"He stayed here for a while," Kate said.

"Let him know I'd like to speak to him."

"He's not returning," Kate said.

"Good riddance, right, mommy?"

Kate leaned over and kissed Ruby's cheek.

"If anything changes for the worse, call me," David offered.

"Troy broke our phone," Ruby said.

David's presence confirmed what Kate already sensed about him. Manly but not macho, friendly with men, shy with women, trustworthy as a practitioner. She regarded him as a *white native*. But unlike others, his conversion had been accepted by the local villagers.

"Thank you for coming," Kate said, wiping her tear-streaked face.

He adjusted his glasses, collected his bag. Kate Ryan was a very attractive woman, he thought. However, casual observation had led him to believe their world-views were incompatible. Her ready smile was the sign of an optimist. He also knew she cultivated healing plants. That alone was optimistic.

"Will you take this?" She handed him a loaf of banana bread and a sack that weighed almost nothing. "Instructions included," she smiled.

David was accustomed to receiving goods in exchange for medical services. Goats, chickens, car parts, plumbing, he was open to barter economy. He bartered for his drugs.

13

The house was cool and dark. A candle burned by the bed, splashing shadows on the walls. When dry lightning flashed, the walls turned silver, the silence broken by bass rumbles in the canyon. Later, it would rain again, soaking the linens on the line.

Kate had tidied the house, thrown out Troy's socks, scrubbed away the noxious remains of Ruby's crisis.

Snuggling into the pillow, Ruby said, "Tell me a story."

The request was a sad reminder that Kate hadn't felt needed by her daughter in a long, long time.

"Tell me a story about daddy," she said, pushing her hip into Kate's side.

Kate closed her eyes. She tried to bring Edwin to mind. There wasn't a clear picture or story but once she started, the story would probably come.

"When your daddy was a little guy with Bepop and Memaw," she said.

Ruby closed her eyes. She could see Bepop and Memaw on their porch in West Oakland. She'd last visited when she was ten. She loved the water, the bridges, the ships chugging across the bay.

"Your daddy loved to fish," Kate said. "Even in the short time I knew him, if he had a free minute, he wanted to fish. I always thought fishing was an excuse to do nothing, but he educated me. He thought it was an art form."

Ruby dozed to the sound of her mother's voice. Her father was the precious missing piece of herself. *Edwin Ryan, Edwin Ryan, Edwin Ryan.* She used to scribble the name everywhere as a way to make him present.

"I believed I had to hold myself up," Kate said warily.

Ruby lay still. Sleep slipped over her.

"I was heavy like you, Ruby. My mind was heavy like yours. It weighed a ton. I didn't know then but I know now. The earth holds us up. Hear me, Ruby? Not our legs or will power or gods but the earth itself if you let it."

Thunder pealed inside the night as the summer rain rinsed and wrung out the air like a giant sheet. There was deep silence. Out of the silent room, a small voice whispered, "Did you love him?"

Kate was startled from sleep herself.

In a voice even smaller, Ruby asked again, "Did you love him?"

"I loved him," Kate sighed painfully.

Ruby didn't let go. "Did you *love* him?"

It was hard for Kate to remember. Hard to separate what was fact from fabrication, the man from the young soldier.

"I got you," Kate said. "That's how much we loved. We *made* you."

Ruby beamed. The answer pleased her. She was an embodiment of love: caramel skin, swampy green eyes, passion for water, a restless nature like her father. Ruby could claim she was almost all Ryan.

14

fter a beer, Troy returned to the central Plaza lined with colonnades: Indians and blankets of jewelry, ropes of red chiles, *ojos de dios*, clothing boutiques, trinkets shops, galleries, Mexican restaurants, and tourists.

With Kate's financial donation, her post office box in Zamora, and a letter from the VA he found in her trash, he opened a checking account at Bank of the West as Edwin Ryan. A few blocks from the bank, he purchased camping supplies and hiked up the Old Pecos Trail past the maze of winding roads, dusty alleys, high adobe walls. He kept walking until he spotted a narrow ungraded driveway with an unused feeling. No security signs, no gates, no well-tended gardens. At the end of the drive were a few downy tamarisks and a half-finished house that looked deserted. He moved swiftly to an arroyo behind the house on the backside of a hill where he climbed, bushwhacked, and climbed.

Troy was hot. The day had taken its toll. He cursed the usual list of malefactors, which began with his father and terminated with the U.S. government. Cursing was not a cure but it provided relief. He scarfed a tin of sardines, a bag of salted peanuts, quaffed his thirst with water and a Coke, stashed his duffle and supplies, leveled a sleeping place, strung up a tarp, and waited for dark.

At nine o'clock, there were still no inhabitants. He jiggled a couple of lopsided windows. The bathroom window was easiest to open. He took a hot shower, shampooed and conditioned his hair, shaved and sprinkled on drops of Chaps, courtesy of his host. He hung his wet towels over the door, borrowed a few items of fresh clothing, and hiked back to town to Jackson's.

It was Ladies' Night. Troy liked women nearby. Their company reassured him. They enabled him to think, better yet to scheme. They proved that whatever his other deficiencies, he succeeded as a man.

"Watch out for the dykes," the bartender grumbled, pushing a beer in his direction.

The bartender was a large flabby man with pomaded gray hair tied neatly in a knot behind his rubbery head, a goatee, silver hoop earrings, and turquoise rings on many fingers.

Troy didn't like his looks. He looked gay himself.

"A mean man can turn a good fucking woman queer," the bartender said. "Or you think they born queer?"

Troy gave a noncommittal nod. He wasn't interested in chitchat. He wanted to relax, nurse his beer, tap his foot to country-and-western classics, and watch couples swing around the center of the floor.

"If you born queer, it makes what ain't natural into natural," the bartender said. "That goes against my beliefs, partner."

When the jukebox burst into a polka, the bar erupted in festivity. Troy was almost overwhelmed by an urge to run up to a thick blond heifer, clamp his hands over her hindquarters, and rodeo her to the ground. He liked the stockiness of her build.

"Built to last," he mumbled happily.

Troy stared but didn't move. From experience he knew women liked to take their time. They liked to work things out for themselves which in the end saved him a lot of trouble. That strategy had worked magic with Kate. If it weren't for her mongrel daughter, he might still be shacked up in Zamora.

"Hi!" the smokey voice said. Her voice was fantastic, breathy and low.

"Hi!" Troy smiled on one side of his mouth.

"Charlene," she said.

"E.R.," he responded. His strong white teeth from Deaf Smith County, Texas, worked their charm.

The two shook hands. Troy thought it peculiar he'd shaken hands twice in one day with women.

"E.R. as in emergency room?" Charlene's thin lips stretched into her cheeks.

Troy smiled with reserve. "As in Edwin Edward Ryan III," he said.

"Who dat?" She grinned with wonderment.

"E.R. blah blah," he laughed.

Confused and impressed, Charlene leaned against the bar and dipped her finger into her vodka tonic. "OK, Mr. Blah Blah," she said, patting her sprayed helmet of blond hair.

"Charlene, you're something." E.R. got right to the point.

In deference, her grin contracted.

"Drinks and dinner, don't that sound like some fun?" He winked at her deep-set animal eyes.

"We're drinking already," she said.

Steady boy, Troy told himself, setting his beer on the bar and sweeping his fingers through his hair. "I guess the flight is catching up with me. Might have to postpone dinner until I settle in this time zone."

"You just got here?" Charlene looped her fingers around his wrist.

"Off the plane a couple of hours ago." Troy consulted his watch. "Had to wait for the limo to drive me up from the Duke. At least, it's not Florida. Takes hours to crawl from the airport."

"You from Florida?"

Troy shrugged. He tilted his chin so the light caught the line of his jaw.

"Daddy needed me to check on the winter palace. It's stinking hot there in summer, but winter's good. Hey, winter is perfect. Golf, fishing, dog races, Gulfstream. Too fucking hot in summer, excuse my French!"

"Like here," Charlene said. "I'm used to living by the ocean. Maybe it gets hot but you can always jump in the water."

"Daddy and his houses," Troy said, echoing the complaints that men of the world always have. Homes here and there, a ski cabin in the mountains, a cottage at the beach, wives and ex-wives, child support, alimony. Besides pleasure, money bought complications.

"I kinda know what you mean," Charlene said. "My problem is my cousin's cats. They keep me going pillar to post."

Charlene didn't look as dumb as she sounded, which made it hard for Troy to know the *right* play. He never really knew. He usually went with his gut.

"I'm staying with my friends, Eagle and Sarah Elderman," he said. "You know them?" He double-checked as if she might.

"I don't know many people," Charlene apologized.

"They had a concert at their kid's school so they dropped me here. They trying like hell to get me to move to Santa Fe. I figure by the end of the week, I'll make up my mind whether to buy a place and order a bed. Or move to Hawaii."

Troy let the sound of his future sink in. He smiled and checked his watch again. "What a pain in the ass airlines are. They wear me out. No direct flights from Palm Beach. I guess I'm saying either I got to high-tail it back to Eagle's hacienda or fall down somewhere. I'm on EST."

"EST?" Charlene gaped. She thought it was a drug.

Troy rubbed his forehead. "You know how jetlag does you," he said.

"I'll give you my phone number and you can call me once you rest up."

"Hey, Charlene! Don't write me off here and now," he said, his eyelids flapping. "*Seize the day*, that's the principle that guided my entire life. Guided my daddy's life too. He could say it in Roman. 'E.R., go out and *carpus diem*.' You know what I mean?"

She had no idea. She retrieved a gum wrapper from her purse and scribbled out her number.

"It means you got to take hold of it when it jumps on your face. If not, it's a life of snooze and lose. Let's say I take your number tonight. Let's say the gum wrapper falls out of my jeans tomorrow. Or the maid doesn't empty my pockets when she does the wash. Then what?"

Charlene knew how tenuous life could be. Of the men who'd taken her number, very few ever called.

"I just moved over here myself," she said, delighted to demonstrate she too could *seize the day*. "If you want, you can come to my place. It's nothing fancy but it's restful and quiet."

Troy's shoulders relaxed. His head drooped with relief. It hadn't been so hard after all.

15

The next afternoon, David Tanner stopped by to check on Ruby.

"*Madame Butterfly*?" he asked as he was leaving.

Kate was preoccupied with a pot of Spanish lavender.

"Would you like to go?"

She looked up. "Where?"

"I'll start over," he smiled. His dating skills had not improved with age. "I have tickets to the opera."

"I heard *Madame Butterfly*." Kate locked the snips and slipped them into her apron.

"Would you care to join me?" he coaxed.

"I'm sure I would," she said. Touched, flattered, embarrassed, it had been a long time since a man asked her to do something civilized.

"Then, shall we?"

"We shall," she teased.

His eyes cleared with relief. "It's gloomy to watch opera alone."

Kate pressed the button of a portable tape deck beside the garden bench. The yard filled with Callas's "*Al dolce guidami castel natio*." She and David clung to the aria as if they were going to shipwreck.

"I didn't know you liked opera," he said.

Kate resented the remark. He didn't know anything about her at all.

"Have you ever heard anyone discuss anything in Zamora except weather and cars?"

"Disease," he laughed. "I assure you disease is a topic of great interest."

Kate laughed too.

"Come to the clinic on Friday at six," he blurted, backing away before Kate Ryan could change her mind.

As David Tanner disappeared, August jumped out of the back of a pickup and loped into the yard.

"How is she?" he cried, licking his furry upper lip.

"Better," Kate said sharply. She still blamed August although she knew he was Ruby's slave. "I'll see if she wants company."

Kate crossed to the house. Ruby's door was shut.

"She's sleeping," Kate reported back.

August's gray eyes blinked. He was hot and thirsty. He had hitched up the mountain. It had taken an hour for someone to stop.

"I brought her this." He reached inside his backpack and pulled out an abalone shell, pitted and dull on one side, opalescent on the other.

"That's kind, August," Kate said.

She held the mollusk in her hand and stroked the nacre. A shell in the desert conjured an entire ocean, the mesas ancient shelves of an ancient sea. Scattered through the mountains were rocks encrusted with shells. Kate kept a collection of those she'd found hiking in the Sandias and Sangre de Cristo ranges.

"Can I wait until she wakes up?" he asked.

A shock ricocheted through Kate as she considered if August and Ruby were lovers.

"We better let her rest," she said.

He sighed desperately. He wanted to know if Ruby blamed him too.

"Give her the shell for me, would you?"

"Of course, August."

"I hope she doesn't think it was my fault."

"Was it?"

"No, the dope was here."

"I believed you yesterday. I still believe you." Kate couldn't help but ask, "Did you tell your mother?"

"No," he said. He told his mother something but it was a lie.

16

Charlene lived in a cheap apartment complex in a neighborhood with ruts for roads and an inordinate number of dogs. A place with more dogs than people always disagreed with Troy. The living room was empty aside from a dozen unpacked cartons and stained wall-to-wall carpet. Charlene pulled out two metal folding chairs, placed them next to a trunk, and lit a jasmine-scented candle. Troy had hoped the place would be as good as a bad motel. But at least it beat the great outdoors.

"Just looking out the window makes you thirsty," she said, opening two beers. "I never been this thirsty. My cousin, he lives across town. We're the same age. We grew up together in San Diego. He paid my way and everything." Charlene's voice hushed. "He's got AIDS. He's dying. Am I talking too much? I *am* talking too much. I haven't had time to fix anything up. Most days I'm over there helping my cousin and keeping him company. Most nights I stay at his place. This is the living room, I guess you can tell. I got my bedroom in there."

Troy spied a mattress on the floor.

"I am dead tired," he announced.

"You look tired," Charlene agreed. "Maybe you wanna watch TV? Whatever's going on inside me, TV sucks it out like voodoo. I love TV." To stop herself from talking, Charlene sunk her teeth into her bottom lip. "I'm sorry," she said.

"Maybe I'll get comfortable," Troy said. "Take off my clothes and crash."

Charlene rushed into the bedroom, swept what was on the mattress to the floor, straightened the bedding, fluffed the pillows, and motioned for Troy to come in.

He kicked off his boots and collapsed.

"Get some rest, E.R. You need it after where you been today."

In the morning, Troy woke refreshed. He watched Charlene sashay by the bed in a diaphanous gown but made no effort to touch her. First of all, she looked better in the dark. In the light he could see acne scars on her face and stains on her teeth. Second, he was already busy at work.

"Hungry?" she asked him.

Of course he was. In a few minutes, an omelet with refried beans, tortillas, and salsa appeared by the bed.

"Did I mention I almost went to San Diego?" He smiled and wiped his toothpick on Charlene's sheet. "My sister Kate lives in La Jolla."

"Ho-ya," Charlene corrected.

"The whole damn house is birch wood with a view that goes to Japan."

"It's pretty there," she agreed. "Not like here. Everything here is brown."

"Honey, if you like green, you should come to Hawaii. Ever been to Maui?"

Charlene shook her head as Troy felt for the photographs in his jacket pocket.

"My family has a condo in Maui. I love it over there. There's a volcano called Hanna-Akala. You can walk down into the crater." He took Charlene's hand. "When my car arrives from Florida, we'll drive into the mountains. If you know where to go, there are spectacular places here."

"I can borrow my cousin's car." Charlene leaned into Troy's shoulder. "He's too sick to drive now."

Troy put his arm around her. He pulled her closer. After a couple of kisses and another cup of coffee, he excused himself. He had an appointment with a realtor.

At the bank, Troy picked up a box of checks. Then, Edwin Ryan went to work. He substituted his old pieces of fake ID with his new name and address. He hired a cab to wait while he bought an HD TV and two VCRs. He duplicated his purchases at a store across town and repeated the maneuver at two computer centers. So far, so good. The fence was reliable. Soon, he'd have a car.

17

Kate excavated a Spanish shawl, a calf-length velvet skirt, a black silk blouse, an antique concho belt, and silver filigree earrings. Classic Southwest fashion brought into vogue in the 1920s by the small international set who surrounded D.H. and Frieda Lawrence when they lived in Taos. Ruby braided her mother's hair into a coil, looping and pinning it with a large silver barrette at the back of her neck.

"Pretty," she said approvingly, dabbing Kate's lips and cheeks with rouge.

Kate lifted her skirt and stepped lightly out of the house, gliding across the yard, turning back to Ruby to wave.

Ruby grinned, happy with her secret. Soon, she'd be gone. That was certain. So far, it was her secret. But Quinn would soon know. She'd written him that morning.

As Kate approached the clinic, she looked at the clouds stretched out in filaments. Gold and red kite strings. The land and sky were consolation for everything. A vast and changing altar.

"Hello, Elaine," Kate said. She wondered if David had discussed Ruby's recent incident.

"We're almost closed unless it's an emergency," Elaine said.

Kate blushed. "David is expecting me."

The doctor and Hector Trujillo emerged from an exam room. Kate glanced from Hector to Elaine. Although impossible to know who knew what, Kate assumed everyone knew everything. Likely Hector had mentioned the showdown with Troy and the scratch on Ruby's cheek. Likely the entire mountain knew about it.

"Kate and I are going to the opera," David announced boyishly. "Do you like opera, Hector?"

"I am sure it is a beautiful thing," he said. "A thing to see before we die, no?"

"You two better get going," Elaine prompted.

Elaine was invaluable to David but her excessive sense of duty made him feel guilty. Then again, everything made him feel guilty. A list that now included his failure to invite Hector Trujillo to the opera.

He stepped aside to let Kate pass down the hall to the back of the clinic into his office.

"You look nice," he said.

Kate nodded appreciatively. "Nice" sounded sincere. She sat in one of the mismatched leather club chairs that faced the doctor's disorderly desk. He slid onto his swivel chair and began to jot notes from his examination of Hector Trujillo. He had ordered a CAT-scan for Hector's lungs. He was worried about Hector.

Kate studied the photographs on the wall of a youthful half-naked David Tanner surrounded by rivers, rapids, waterfalls.

"You're a brave soul," she said.

"It looks scary but . . ." He eyeballed the picture of his matchstick kayak in the pounding rapids of Lava Falls. "No, it *is* scary. I mean, it depends. If it's Lava Falls and the Colorado, it's serious. Lava Falls is a ten."

His modesty surprised her.

"On the Colorado, the rapids are in a class of their own. Ten is mother of mothers." He sighed with pleasure. "Once in the arms of the river, the river master says, *Flow is the only way to go*."

Kate sighed too, recalling the happy outings on the Salmon with Ruby and her cousins. Mostly flat water, nothing very scary.

After he finished his notes and shut down the computer, David checked the lock on the Phoenix floor safe. He locked his bar refrigerator and file cabinets. He bolted the window and chained his outside door.

"Expecting someone?" Kate smiled. She never locked anything.

"I was recently robbed," he said.

Shock registered on Kate's face. Activity in the local underground economy included counterfeiters, heroin and pot importers, meth manufacturers, a variety of illegal goods, and caravans of undocumented transients. However, robbery went against local code. It was disrespectful to take a poor man's money or things. People got drunk and drove off mountain roads. Or sickened to death from pesticides in the orchards and fields. Or overdosed on drugs. Or got fatally shot. But robbery was extremely rare.

"They copped some drugs," David shrugged. "I try to keep a good supply on hand."

Kate knew the farmers and their families depended on Dr. Tanner. They protected him. They would never steal from him. "But who?"

"Teenagers," he said.

18

It was dusk in the valley. Shades of lavender settled in the cottonwoods while the mountaintops flamed. As David and Kate drove down the mountain, Troy and Charlene headed up. Along the curves of the road, they watched the sun's reflection over the cliffs and crags.

"Beautiful," Troy mused. He was drawn to the high peaks and far vistas. He was also pleased with his success. The past few days had netted several thousand dollars, tax-free, and fully insured by the FDIC.

"You happy, baby?" Charlene asked.

Troy's teeth gleamed in the rays of sun.

"E.R.?" Charlene burrowed into his ribs.

"Yes, baby."

"Don't you think it's time we get to know each other better?" Her smokey voice still aroused him.

"Sure, baby," he whispered. "It's our time now."

So far, Troy had only slept in Charlene's bed and eaten her simple meals. He had had a lot on his mind with business and until his mind was clear, he wasn't good for anything else.

Charlene hadn't complained. During the day, she was at her cousin's house. At night, she was tired too. She was grateful for the company. It was the first semblance of a boyfriend in a couple of years.

Up the highway past Zamora was an unmarked fire road into the Pecos National Forest. When he stayed at Kate's, Troy sometimes walked the road. Once he went with a neighbor's wagon and mule to haul firewood. Like the estovers in ancient law, fallen wood was available for anyone to haul away.

Troy followed the lane past the groves of aspen, scrub juniper, pine. He skirted a large depression where an underground spring spilled into a pool of watercress. The light deepened to iridescent purple as hundreds of bats dove and darted like arrows across the soggy meadow.

Charlene used her Swiss Army knife to break the seal of a California champagne. She lit a votive candle and placed it on the dashboard of the car.

"I'm feeling no pain," she sighed, throwing her breasts into Troy's face.

"*No pain, no gain*," he chortled. "Daddy instilled that in us."

"I'm glad he wasn't my daddy," Charlene said.

"Me too," Troy hugged her. "They arrest people for that. Anyway I already got one sister."

"How is she?" Charlene had heard lots of stories about E.R.'s sister, Kate. Her first husband had been killed in the Gulf War.

"It's her husband," Troy said. "They got bad news today."

"I'm sorry." Charlene put her hand protectively over his. She was empathetic to a fault.

"Brain tumor," he said soberly, thinking how harmless it was. The words were only stories and would soon disappear.

"Isn't he a brain surgeon?" Charlene's face crumpled.

"They say it's usually your work that kills you."

"Two husbands dead, that's sad."

"I may have to go out and take care of things." He squeezed Charlene's fingertips and brought them to his lips.

"I knew you were gonna say that."

"Do for them what you do for your cousin here." His fingers ran up and down Charlene's neck and skipped playfully across her breasts. "But not too soon, not until we get to know each other better."

They laughed, relaxed and warmed by the wine. The candlelight was golden. Outside, a star fell across the deep moonlit blue.

Charlene rummaged in the backseat for a blanket. She sprang out of the car and beckoned him to follow. They wandered to a flat sunken spot on the perimeter of the meadow. Troy brushed away the small rocks and spread the cover on the ground, setting his boots and a second bottle of champagne at the corners.

"Intoxicating," he said, smelling the crushed sage.

Charlene dropped to her knees. He stood, contemplating the dark roots of her hair in the moonlight and a bald spot at the crown.

"How is it you like to make a man happy?" he whispered.

"Different ways," she said, touching the bulge in his jeans.

"How about one way? Then another?" He was feeling saucy.

"You mean a nibble?" Charlene asked, easing him out of his pants.

She spread her lips on the tip of his penis. She circled the tip with her tongue. She took him through her mouth behind her teeth into her throat where her tongue undulated like a harem dancer's belly.

"Don't stop! Don't stop!" He moaned until he exploded and collapsed on the blanket beside her. For several minutes he lay panting, genuinely awed.

"You *do* know something, baby," he finally said.

"I know how he wants it," she said, pressing Troy's hand inside her blouse, rubbing his fingers around her nipples, directing his hand down her belly until it reached the tufts of her coarse pubic hair.

In one motion, he yanked off her clothes. But as he readied himself to pounce, he paused. In the glassy light of the moon he scanned the scarred body beneath him. Its anatomy slightly misplaced.

Charlene saw a question and answer pass between his eyes.

"What are you?" he seethed.

"Baby," she crooned, scuttling backwards across the blanket. "It's me, Charlene. It's only me."

"Fucking freak," he croaked and leapt toward her.

He seized her elbow and swung, planting a brick-hard jab into the bridge of her nose and breaking it. Then, dragging her by her bleached hair to the edge of the watercress pool, with both hands around her neck, he pushed her head below the water and counted to one hundred.

19

Troy's feelings about killing were different than other crimes. Other crimes were moves in a game. They came with inherent dangers, but they were only violations of manmade law. They required luck and finesse. In killing, however, he experienced no high. Killing disgusted him. Breaking Charlene's nose, he remembered. Dragging her body, he remembered. But after he reached the pond, there was a blank except for her bloody face and blurred eyes wavering inches below the water's surface. He didn't believe he killed her. He was in a state of total disbelief, afraid that what couldn't be true might trick him. He'd been tricked before. A picture rose out of his mother's Bible of a sword and angel ready to smite him as soon as he stood up. He lay on the ground semiconscious, trying to escape the incontrovertible.

An hour passed before he wrapped the body in the blanket and carried it from the meadow into the aspen grove. With his boots he carved out a crude indentation in the ground. He dug deeper with a pointed rock. He put Charlene inside the shallow cradle and covered her with dirt and duff.

Troy was wired. His heart raced. He had to work out a new story, a new set of circumstances, moving as quickly as possible before the old story and circumstances caught up with him.

At the car, he removed his filthy clothes. He bundled them in plastic ripped from Charlene's cousin's dry cleaning. He put on the cousin's clean pressed clothes. He checked the gas gauge. He kicked the tires. Charlene's cousin's car was only a year old with less than fifteen hundred miles. He unlocked the glove compartment and found a nine millimeter pistol and vehicle registration for Robert Russo. It felt like his car now.

He drove along the fire road without headlights. When he hit the highway, he turned north on the back road to Taos. After less than a mile, he turned on his lights and headed back to Zamora.

The highway wound around the mountain toward the village. He passed the bullet-punctured sign—ZAMORA. It was after ten but the mercantile store was still open. A light shone over the front porch of the clinic. Pick-ups idled at the side of the church.

Troy pulled into Kate's drive. He could use a word of encouragement, a shower, a beer, a bowl of chile and tortillas. He intended to repay the cash he borrowed plus interest. Maybe Kate would even be glad to see him.

He strode to the house, one pocket stuffed with money, the other with a small firearm. He ran the hose over his hands, splashed his face, pushed on the door. He looked at the tidy empty room. Decidedly emptier and tidier without him.

"Kate!" he called.

Ruby appeared from her room, scowling. "What do you want?"

"Where's your mother?"

"None of your fucking business."

"I guess I'll wait and make it my fucking business." He walked to the fridge and removed the six-pack of Coors he'd bought the week before. He found crackers, cheese, peanuts.

"I got my money from Texas," he said, taking a roll from his pants and throwing it and the gun on the bed. "IRS suspended its lien." Troy looked to see if he was making an impression. "I decided to drop in before I left for Maui."

"Nice," Ruby boiled, glancing at his attire. Maybe Hawaiian style, maybe not. A blue dress shirt with a silk-screened photo of Elton John on the pocket, double-creased dress slacks two inches too short, and dirty boots.

"I thought your mom might think so. I brought $450, enough to get the phone fixed."

"My mom feels sorry for strays," Ruby smirked.

"You got an ugly fucking mouth, you know that?"

"Did you come back for your dope too?"

"What dope?"

"The fucking poison you hid in my mom's sewing machine."

Troy had almost forgotten his escapade at the clinic.

"It wasn't even pot, dummy," Ruby taunted.

"Of course it was." There he went, slipping up.

"Dr. Tanner checked it out. It was smack and shit."

That was a surprise.

"Dr. Tanner said it was bad shit."

"He should know. It was his smack, his shit."

"They'll be back soon. You can ask him."

An image of Charlene sucking him off flashed, followed by a cramp in his fingers as he held her under water. Lightning, then thunder.

"What you mean *they*?" He pinned Ruby against the wall.

Her face contorted. "They went to the opera."

"Your mom with the doctor?" Troy asked incredulously. *Kate the slut was already fucking the Jew doctor?* He hoped he didn't have to kill David Tanner too.

20

Ruby sat on her bed. Beside her was her duffle packed with everything she needed. Eighty-four dollars was in her bra. The door was locked, but the hasp was a joke. Nothing more than a symbol of privacy. A mouse could break the lock.

She dragged the bag to the window and pushed aside the curtain. The frame didn't rise more than a few inches, but if Troy broke the door, she planned to dive through the glass and run. She planned to wake Hector Trujillo and his brother. Or dash to a phone and call the sheriff. Or hide by the road and wait for David Tanner's car.

A half-hour passed. Her mind fluctuated between schemes of escape and submission to doom. She counted backwards from a hundred in English and Spanish, trying to reduce herself to a number. She was on one side of an equation, and as long as the distance between two bodies, hers and Troy's, stayed constant, she was safe.

Eventually, the counting and waiting dissolved into futile exercises. She tried to raise the window again. The dry wood cracked but the window didn't budge. She crouched on the floor, listening. Then, steadily putting her weight forward, she tiptoed to the door, unhitched the lock, and peered into the living room.

Troy was on his back, lightly snoring. His boots were by the bed, their soles caked with mud, the leather casings soaked with water. Empty cans of beer lay on the floor. Tracks of mud crisscrossed the polished planks and Kate's prized Navajo rugs.

Ruby zeroed in on the money and the gun. She crawled to the bed and crammed some bills into her jeans. Then she reached for the gun. Stubby, lightweight, comfortable. She had a terrific case of jitters. But with the gun in her hand, fright conflated with elation.

Troy groaned and turned over. "Kate," he called, waking slowly.

He reached across the quilt for his money and shoved it into Charlene's cousin's slacks. He fondled the pillow for the gun. He looked on the floor at his boots.

"Ruby!" he yelled.

In the darkest corner of her room, Ruby hunched down and aimed the gun at the door. She heard Troy stumble out the front, open and slam car doors, stumble back into the house, banging, rattling, cursing.

She crept to the bedroom door. She stooped and looked through the keyhole. Kate's bed was torn apart, the garbage can turned upside down, the refrigerator open, the kitchen shelves cleared, the drawers dumped.

Troy stood dejected. Part exhaustion, part alcohol, part confusion.

When Ruby appeared in the doorway, he was surprised.

"I thought you were gone," he said.

"I'm going now."

"Off to Idaho in the middle of the night?"

"Far away from here." Ruby's jade-green eyes focused on the front door.

"Your mom know?"

With her bag slung over her shoulder and Troy's gun behind her back, Ruby skipped past the bed.

"What you got there?" he hissed.

He lunged as she ran into the garden.

"You fucking bitch!" he screamed as she streaked to the road. It was only a hundred more yards to the Trujillo farm.

Even barefoot, it was easy to take her down. Troy twisted her arm behind her. But as he balled his fist to punch her, Charlene's bloodied face appeared like a ghost. Before Ruby could think, in reaction to the pain, she squeezed her right hand. She didn't look or aim. Only the report told her she had fired.

"Fuck-ing bitch," he slurred in slow thick syllables as he fell to the ground.

Ruby heard a cry and a curse but she didn't turn around. She ran to Troy's car, jumped in, turned the key, and drove away.

21

There was no mayor in Zamora. There was a county sheriff, county commissioners, county boards and departments where Zamora was hardly represented. There was also a water collaborative in the village where grievances over irrigation could be addressed. Elected or not, Hector Trujillo played the role of village chief.

At half past eleven, he heard a shot from the direction of the Ryan place. He ran madly, arriving just as an unfamiliar late-model car skidded onto the road. He did not see the driver but the moonlight was strong enough to note the license number.

Nearby, he found the man he knew to be Kate Ryan's lover lying in the portion of yard used for parking. Kate's car was in its usual spot. There was no sign of her or Ruby.

"I'm hurt," Troy wept.

Hector leaned over the deflated body and crossed himself. "You hit?"

Troy rolled on his back. Hector saw that blood had soaked the man's slacks midway down his left leg and spread on the ground.

"I'm bleeding to death for sure," he groaned.

"No, no," Hector said to comfort him. "You be fine."

Hector rushed into Kate's house. It was in total disarray. He snatched pillows, towels, blankets, sheets.

"Ruby!" he called. "Kate!"

No answer. Maybe they were shot too.

Returning outside, he propped up Troy's leg, tucked a blanket around his body, stanched the wound with a ripped towel.

"Thanks a lot," Troy mumbled. He'd never liked Mexicans but Hector had come in handy.

"Where's Ruby?" Hector asked.

"Little fucker shot me."

Hector didn't believe it for a minute. The wounded man was in a state of delirium. Hector would wait. He would not press for details.

"I going to find Dr. Tanner and call emergency, okay?"

Troy blinked. He could use a big shot of morphine.

Hector did a quick sweep of the house and grounds but turned up nothing. No body, no gun, no sign of blood. Only emptied drawers and strewn garbage.

"Thank you, Jesús," Hector exclaimed, crossing himself.

At that moment, David Tanner and Kate were returning from the opera and a late supper on Canyon Road. Both were giddy from an evening of Puccini and several glasses of wine. Across from the entrance to the Ryan place, David's high beams illuminated a spectral Hector Trujillo, waving frantically.

David lurched to a stop. "What?"

"Ruby?" Kate panicked.

"A man," Hector hesitated, confused how to identify Troy.

"Ruby!" Kate flung open the car door and started to run.

Hector Trujillo shrugged with shame.

"Get in," David ordered.

Troy lay under the blanket, bawling, "Fucking cunt bitch! Fucking freak bitch!"

"Troy!" Kate stared as if he'd risen from the dead.

David kneeled beside him. He ordered Hector to fetch an emergency kit from the trunk, boil a pot of water, bring more towels from the house.

"Where's Ruby?" Kate's eyes cursed Troy.

He didn't answer. He watched David Tanner slice off the leg of Charlene's cousin's pants and palpate the area around the knee. He almost fainted from the pain.

David assessed the wound. The bullet had grazed the patella but the kneecap wasn't shattered.

"Ruby?" Kate wanted to strangle him.

"Bitch shot me," Troy said slow and low.

"What'd you say?" David demanded.

"Ruby shot me."

"That's not true!" Kate said.

Coruscating moonlight drenched the cars, the tool shed, the chicken coop. Kate ran around the yard. "Ruby! Ruby!" she shouted. At the sight of the front room, she gagged.

Hector stood at the stove, waiting for water to boil and casting an eye at Kate Ryan. He knew what it was to have trouble in the blood. One of his brothers killed his own wife. Two nephews were in prison.

"Kate," he said with all the kindness in his heart, "Ruby is not here."

"Troy said Ruby shot him."

"He said same thing to me. But he's crazy with pain. He doesn't know what he saying. I saw who shot him. I saw with my own eyes."

"Who?" Kate struggled through the sobs.

"Somebody in a new car, a white dusty car. Maybe Honda Accord. I never seen this car anywhere. It didn't come from Zamora." Hector tapped his forehead, "I took down the license number."

"Who? Who was in the car?"

"It was my misfortune not to see the driver."

"Kidnapped," Kate burst out.

"I think only one was in the car."

"In the trunk or on the floor," Kate cried.

She stepped around the mess. A fight had obviously occurred. Kate suddenly understood. She sprang through the front door and bounded to Troy's side.

"Can you give me something, doc?" he asked.

"The house is wrecked," she waved. "Somebody went in there to find something. It's only one thing."

"What?" David asked as he washed and dressed the wound.

"Something for pain," Troy said.

Kate gulped back the tears. "Him!" She jabbed Troy's chest. "You put those drugs inside my sewing machine, didn't you?"

Troy couldn't think straight with a throbbing knee. The knee consumed him.

"He stored his drugs here. Whoever came knew that. They tore up the house and kidnapped Ruby."

"That sounds right," Hector nodded. "I only saw the car. It was going very fast. But I got the license plate number in my head."

Kate rose to full size. Her devotion to kindness, her compassion for suffering, her quest for a spiritual life, evaporated. She put her foot on Troy and pressed.

"Who took Ruby?" she demanded.

When he looked up, he saw Charlene's busted face swinging from the cottonwood. "You crazy bitch! I'm saying she shot me!"

"Were those your drugs?" David asked him.

"Nobody been here but her and me. She shot me. She took my car. That's the story."

"What car?"

"My money came from Texas so I brought back your cash."

Kate clasped her hands over her heart. She sank to the ground and folded her knees beneath her, raising her eyes to the brightest moon in the history of the world and imploring Selene, goddess of the moon, Mary, Jesus, Kwan Yin, and Krishna, intoning their names over and over. Drugs, cars, guns, money, none of it mattered. Only Ruby mattered.

22

At the clinic, David notified the county sheriff's office and New Mexico state police. It was past three in the morning but the officer assured him a bulletin would be issued immediately. David relayed the license plate number of the car and a description of Ruby Ryan, missing and possibly kidnapped. He promised to drop off her photograph at state police headquarters in Santa Fe.

"Anything wrong?" Elaine startled him.

"I didn't know you were here."

"I spend every moment here," she said wearily.

"I'm trying to fix a nightmare over at the Ryan place," David said.

A smile flitted through Elaine's eyes. She knew Kate Ryan was trouble.

"Anything I can do?" Unlike David Tanner she relished emergencies.

"The drifter up there has been shot. Ruby Ryan is missing."

Elaine clapped her hand over her mouth. "I'll get dressed," she said.

David collapsed at his desk enveloped by the stillness of night. It was dark and still. The moon had dipped over the horizon. He poured himself a shot of Jack and stuck the bottle in his satchel. Hector and Kate could probably use a drink. He gathered painkillers and a hypodermic of morphine, then drove back to Kate's, hoping a miracle had brought Ruby home.

After Troy had been sedated, David suggested they make a litter with a board and transport him into the house.

"Can't we go?" Kate asked.

"The sheriff's coming. He'll be here in an hour or less. The state police has wired the license plate to all points." He rested his hand on Kate's shoulder. "There's nothing to do right now. We don't know if she was kidnapped. We don't know which direction they went. She could have wandered off with a friend. Doesn't she sometimes sleep in the truck?"

"This is different," Kate broke down. "In a few hours, she could be across the border. She could be anywhere."

"In a few minutes, the license number and her photo will be at every police station and outpost in the country. They'll find her," David declared grimly.

By dawn, the village had been invaded by a fleet of law enforcement. Hector Trujillo assumed his place as spokesman. Other villagers stood respectfully by the road fifty yards from the house, staring at the facade. In awe, they listened as Hector explained how drug thugs came to Kate's house, shot Troy, and kidnapped Ruby. He added it was he who *captured* the license number.

During the interview with police, Kate fell apart over the simplest of questions. It made her ache to think how beautiful her Ruby was.

"What was Ruby wearing when you last saw her?"

"*Last*?" The question caused her to fall into David's arms.

When Troy awoke, it was eight o'clock. His knee throbbed. He was dizzy. He wondered who the men in and out of uniform were. Better not to know, he concluded, diving back into opiated semiconsciousness.

"I think we can rouse him," David said.

Troy recognized the Jew doctor's voice.

A deputy touched Troy's arm. "Awake?"

Troy blinked in confusion. "What happened?"

"That's what we'd like to know," the state police inspector said. "What can you tell us?"

On the one hand, there was the question of bad checks. On the other, Charlene.

"Everything," he grunted.

"How about bringing the man some coffee?" The inspector waved to a subordinate. "Troy Mason, is it?"

"This really hurts," he said, touching his leg, grateful the pain gave his brain an edge.

"The doctor will give you another shot as soon as we get your story down. We need your mind as clear as possible."

Troy sank into the pillow and sipped the lukewarm coffee.

"Where you boys want me to begin?"

"Last night," the inspector said.

Troy spoke in thoughtful measured sentences. "I got here late," he said.

"From where?"

"I drove up from Santa Fe, thinking Kate would be home. She and I, we used to have a little thing," he added sheepishly. "I wanted to see her because she helped me when I was down. She gave me a place to stay. She lent me money. She did other nice things for me," he blushed.

He sounded sincere. If anything, the inspector thought *too* sincere.

"When I got hold of my own money, first thing crossed my mind was repaying Kate. I rented a car and drove straight here. Ruby was home. She told me her mom went off with the doctor," Troy frowned. "Of course, that ain't my business. It might have been my business once," he paused regretfully. "A day or two ago."

"We weren't together like that," Kate protested. "We weren't a couple."

The inspector interrupted, "What happened after you arrived last night?"

"Ruby was never friendly to me. She treated me poorly, the way she treats everything. I didn't take it personally since she's going through a *rough* time."

"What do you mean *rough*?"

"Like disturbed."

The inspector turned to Kate. "Is that true?"

"She's a teenager," Kate said. "She has ups and downs."

"Ruby told me I could wait. She told me her mom would be home around eleven. Eleven came and went. I figured Kate and the doctor took a liking to each other."

"That's not true," David Tanner objected.

"I laid my debt on the bureau over there with extra for interest." Troy faced the corner with a puzzled look. "There was a pile of money there last night but they probably got it."

"They?" the inspector prodded.

"Two hippie types come in here, demanding to see Ruby. I guess they were friends of hers."

"Can you describe them?"

"They had on masks but they were white boys. I could see their hands. They had long blond hair." Troy searched for the right words. "Their clothing was filthy like animals."

"Were they armed?"

Troy assessed things were going well. "One had a sawed-off shotgun. The other pulled a pistol when I tried to stop them from taking the girl."

"What did they want?"

"Either dope or their cut. I butted in like I shouldn't. I told them Ruby wasn't dealing. She might have problems at school. Problems with her mom but you can understand why. She's the only," he groped for the exact expression, "the only half-colored person around here. If anything like dealing was going on, I'd have known it when I was living here. So would Kate. Right, baby?"

"Ruby is not a drug dealer," Kate said indignantly.

The sheriff and inspector were confounded. They'd already heard from the doctor and Hector Trujillo that Troy swore the girl shot him. They asked David to step outside. They called Hector over and let them repeat their version of events.

"He said Ruby shot him. But it don't make sense." Hector's dark eyes bugged. "He spoke ungodly things about her. Things I would never say to nobody."

Inside the house, the sheriff went to Troy's side. He patted him on the head. It was a paternal gesture from a large powerful man. "Did you tell Dr. Tanner and Mr. Trujillo that Ruby Ryan shot you?" he asked.

"Did I?" Troy sighed. His eyes swept the room, rolling from face to face, searching and beseeching. "I must have really been out of my mind."

23

By midmorning a small crowd had gathered in the Ryan yard, the Spanish farmers around Hector Trujillo, the gringos beside Elaine.

"You remember the man living here? You probably saw him around?" Elaine tried not to sound judgmental.

"Kate Ryan's boyfriend?" a woman asked.

"We saw him," the mechanic said. "He fixes cars."

"I thought he was a narc," someone added.

"Kate knows how to pick them," Elaine said. "He was shot last night."

"Killed?"

"I heard it was Ruby who shot him."

"Drug dealers shot him," a teacher chimed in.

"Is he dead?"

"Not dead. He's talking to police but Ruby is missing."

August came up on the last word. He'd spent the night with a friend in Ojo Sarco and decided to stop at the Ryan place on his way home. He was shocked by the sight of police cars and an ambulance in the driveway. Nothing ever happened in Zamora.

"What the hell!" he exclaimed.

"Someone shot Kate Ryan's boyfriend, Troy."

"He's not her boyfriend," August said.

"Maybe not but he's shot. Ruby's gone."

"Gone?"

"Kidnapped."

"Not true!" August declared heatedly.

"Maybe true, maybe not," someone offered sympathetically.

"Those kids grew up together," the mechanic explained.

"Strangers came, shot the man, and took Ruby. That's the unconfirmed story so far," Elaine said.

"No way!"

"Ask Hector Trujillo. He was the first to get here."

August walked unsteadily over to the village farmers. They stood, passing around cans of Bud tall boys. Behind them was a patch of fields. A cow had managed to escape through the fence and grazed by the road. Beyond the fields was the Trujillo compound and satellite dish. Among the men was Juan Pedro, who recently told Ruby she had nice tits and asked if he could smell her hair.

August walked directly up to Juan Pedro and punched him in the jaw.

"Hey!" Juan Pedro jumped on August and pounded his back. "Fucking dog *mierda*!"

Two others pulled the boys apart.

"Is it true Ruby's gone?" August stammered.

"It is true," Hector replied.

Tears clouded August's eyes. Somehow this had to be partly his fault.

"He makes Ruby's life miserable," August accused Juan Pedro. "Every day he says ugly shit to her."

"Hey, you!" an officer shouted across the yard.

"Who me?" Hector started to run.

"No, the kid." The officer motioned for August to step forward.

"Hello, August," David Tanner said.

"If I can assist," the young man fumbled. "You know I'd do anything."

The inspector pointed to Kate's wicker armchair. "Tell us where you were last night."

"Where?" August laughed nervously. "Asleep, I guess."

"Coffee, August?" Kate asked.

"Last night?" the inspector repeated sternly. "Were you home?"

"I was at Wayne's house in Ojo Sarco."

"Did you see Ruby?"

"I wanted to," he said.

The inspector rose. He towered over August. "Why didn't you?"

"She doesn't want to see me." August kept his head down, his eyes on the floor.

"Did you two have a fight?"

"Ask if the Wayne dude has a blond ponytail?" Troy interrupted.

"Not a fight exactly. Sometimes, she's moody. I can't ever tell what's going through her mind."

"Do you know that man there?" The inspector pointed to Kate's bed.

August's eyebrows arched. "Sure I know him. I wish I didn't."

"Mr. Mason says two guys your age, your height, your hair color came by last night."

August laughed too loudly. "He's lying!"

"Better watch it, punk-ass hippie bastard liar!" Troy yelled.

"Why would you accuse Mr. Mason of lying?"

"He's the liar!" Troy bellowed. "He and Ruby both, they're dope fiends. Ask him. Stealing dope and lying about what they do, staying out all night, drinking, getting high, fucking and sleeping in a truck. Ask him!"

"Why would you say that about Mr. Mason?"

"I don't know. I don't know why I said it. I guess Ruby told me he's a liar. Like pathological liar. Like somebody who makes up stories and lives in a fantasy world."

"Why would Ruby say that about Mr. Mason?"

"Because he's always banging on about his money and his cars and his yachts and his houses everywhere. He carries around photos of shit and says they belong to him. But it's like he cut them out of *Vanity Fair.* He wants to impress everybody while he sponges off Kate. Ruby saw through him. I guess I did too."

"Was it a lie?" Troy cried. "Didn't I get my money and come up here to pay Kate back?"

Kate stood up. "Can you leave now and look for Ruby?"

"We're looking," the inspector said dryly. "We got lots of folks looking."

His opinions had vacillated wildly since he arrived at the Ryan household.

"August, do you know where Ruby is now?" he asked.

"Of course not," August said unconvincingly.

"If you know, August," Kate sobbed. "I could die of worry right now."

"I don't know anything," he said feebly.

"Put a mask on his face and tell me he doesn't know anything," Troy said.

"What does *that* mean?" August asked.

"Doc, my knee is killing me." Troy tried to move his leg.

"The ambulance will run you down to the hospital in Santa Fe," the inspector responded. "How does that sound?"

Troy closed his eyes to savor the question. It sounded like the Hand of the Lord had joined him in a master plan.

24

state police officer telephoned August's mother to report her son had been detained for questioning in a shooting. He refused to discuss anything more.

"I have a right to know," Lorna Young grumbled. "He's a minor."

"August is at the Ryan residence in Zamora. He hasn't been charged."

"Charged?" she exploded.

Lorna slammed down the receiver and sped up the mountain. She arrived as the ambulance with Troy lumbered onto the blacktop road.

"What the hell is going on?" she shouted to the vigilant bystanders.

"Kate Ryan's boyfriend was shot last night," Elaine said. "They think it was drug dealers who came and took Ruby."

"Horseshit!" Lorna stormed into the house, her head thrust forward, her eyes bulging.

Lorna Young was a large, freckled redhead who earned a handsome livelihood as a gallery owner in Santa Fe. Like Kate Ryan, she'd been raised in New England, educated at private schools, and traveled west to California in a caravan. Like Kate, finding New Mexico was a fortuitous accident.

"What the hell is going on?" she demanded.

"And you are?" the inspector asked.

"August's mother," the sheriff answered.

"Lorna Young, mother of August Young-Ratcliffe," she said belligerently.

"Mom!" August whined.

"I was told my son is being *detained*."

"That's incorrect," the sheriff said.

"I was told my son is being *detained*," Lorna said. "I would like to know why. If you cannot tell me, I will take him home."

"Mom!"

"A man has been shot, Mrs. Young. He tells us two young Anglo men were the perpetrators. Your son may be able to help identify them."

"And Ruby is missing!" August sniveled. "Maybe kidnapped!"

"Horseshit!" Lorna Young expectorated.

"What makes you say that, Mrs. Young?"

Lorna squirmed. "Where is Kate Ryan?"

"Resting in the other room."

"Then I'll be frank."

"Please," the inspector prompted.

"I think Ruby got in some kind of trouble and fled."

"Why would you think that?"

"Because I've known the girl all her life."

"No, mom."

"Born under the sign of trouble. You don't have to believe in astrology to know it's true."

"Not true!" August protested.

"Shut up, August!" she commanded. "For years she has been intent on involving my son in drink, drugs, sex experiments, and ruin. Kate Ryan's philosophy is free rein. As a result Ruby has had no direction, no guidance, no parenting." Lorna paused to take a breath, "The girl's out of control."

Kate appeared in the doorway to Ruby's room.

"I can swear my son had nothing to do with this."

"Lorna, I have no idea why you hate us," Kate said.

The inspector signaled for his assistant to bring over more coffee.

"My child is missing," Kate trembled. "That's the only issue of importance here."

"True," the inspector agreed.

He looked at each of the mothers, grief-stricken Kate Ryan and combative Lorna Young. His hunch that August and Ruby conspired in a plot against Kate's boyfriend had become increasingly plausible. The duffle bag they found in the driveway filled with Ruby's things tended to confirm it. Even her toothbrush was in the bag. Why she didn't take it, where she went, who shot Troy and tore up the house, these remained mysteries. Nevertheless, he was convinced he would know Ruby's whereabouts within the hour.

"Mrs. Young, you seem so certain Ruby wasn't kidnapped. Is there a reason?" the inspector asked.

"Of course, there's a reason. I don't go around making things up," Lorna said.

"Well?" The inspector tapped his foot.

All eyes were on her.

"I saw her," she confessed.

"Louder, please."

"I saw her late last night."

"Why didn't you say so? Why didn't you spare me one less minute of agony?"

Lorna blinked back tears of agitation. It seemed Kate Ryan's moral position was indisputably right.

"Where did you see her?" the inspector asked.

"She came to my house."

"What time was that?"

"After midnight."

"And?" the inspector asked impatiently.

"She came to see August. I told her he wasn't home."

"Was he?" the sheriff interjected.

"He was at a friend's house," Lorna said.

"What friend?"

"I told you," August said.

"I'm talking to your mother. What friend?"

"I'm not sure," Lorna said. "Maybe Justin, maybe Wayne. Why don't you ask August?"

"Was Ruby alone?" For the inspector, this question was of utmost importance.

"I don't know," Lorna said.

"How did she arrive at your house?"

"She was driving a car I didn't recognize. In the moonlight, I could see it was a new model. She was upset August wasn't home. We only spoke for a minute. I tried to coax her inside but she didn't want to talk to me. She wrote, *Leaving for good, going forever*. Now I realize I should have tried to stop her but she was anxious to go."

The inspector refreshed his coffee. He slowly stirred in a spoon of raw sugar. "You said, '*Wrote*'?"

"Did I?"

"You said, '*Wrote*.'"

"I meant," Lorna's brash confidence fell away. "She gave the impression she was in a hurry to get somewhere."

"You said, '*Wrote*.'"

"She wrote August a note, *Leaving for good*," Lorna said. "I found it this morning."

"Mrs. Young, do you have the note from Miss Ryan in your possession?"

"No, I don't."

"Can we take you home to get the note?" the inspector asked although he'd already decided the question was moot, the note bogus. The woman would perjure herself to protect her son.

Lorna hung her head. "I burned it. I'm sorry, August."

August's eyes flamed with hate.

"I burned it because she called me a 'bitch.' I didn't want my son to read that. She's already done so much harm to our family."

The inspector gave his most plausible theory one more try.

"August, do you know where Ruby Ryan is?"

Lorna Young jumped out of her chair. "Of course, he doesn't! I told you, I saw her! She drove off! She panicked, I told you!"

The inspector turned to August, "Do you know where Ruby is?"

August dropped his head in his hands and mumbled, "If there was anything I could do, anything I could tell you, I would." He lifted his face of misery. "I was at Wayne's house all night. I know nothing, nothing at all."

25

Unfortunately, it was not Hector Trujillo or his brothers who found Charlene's corpse. If they had, the news of Ruby's death that raced through Zamora could have been avoided. Instead, it was the oldest villager, toothless and half-blind, out loading his wagon with wood. He came across the partly naked and battered body of a young woman in a shallow grave.

After the old man reported the information to Elaine, she delivered it to the police inspector. Heaving up the words with genuine grief, she whispered, "They found Ruby's body in the woods."

The inspector moved swiftly to the circle of Spanish farmers camped at the side of the road, beer cans and rosaries in hand and heads bowed in prayer.

"Who saw the body?" he asked gruffly.

"Myself," the eldest in the group admitted. Weathered in the cheeks like buffalo leather, his tongue thumped against his gums.

"Where?"

The old man pointed north. Another described the fire road that led to the meadow with the spring-fed pond.

"Get an ambulance up here," the inspector shouted to an assistant. "Radio the sheriff to come back."

Through the window, Kate watched the commotion. After Elaine entered the house and repeated what she knew to David Tanner, Kate saw him blanche. She felt Elaine's hand settle heavily on her shoulder.

"What?" she turned to David.

Quicker better, he thought. "They found a body."

"No!" she moaned, flinging Elaine aside.

"No!" she defied God.

"No!" The word spreading infernal darkness, poison, lamentation, and grief over the land.

"No!" she refused to believe.

"No!" she pleaded to every deity invented by man: Tara for compassion, Buddha for detachment, Kali for destruction, Jesus for salvation,

Yahweh for revenge, and the mysteries who govern the physical laws of the universe.

"No!" The mantra of a madwoman who rejected witness, rumor, and report until she had bona fide proof.

Kate streaked across the yard, tackling the inspector.

"I'm coming with you! I'm coming too!"

David ran after her. "Let me go, Kate. You stay. I'm going."

He was crying as he propped her against the car, kissing her hand, trying to break the terror down into something small and tender.

Kate flung open the door of the patrol car. She challenged them to refuse her.

"I'm here," David said. "I'm here beside you."

Three miles north of Zamora, two state police cars and the sheriff's truck turned onto a seldom used and barely maintained fire road. The ride was slow and bumpy. They parked and began to walk along the road. Fine mocha-colored dust coated their shoes and clothes.

Kate was the first to spot a limp female body. Even at a distance, she could see it wasn't Ruby. She fell to her knees and began to vomit.

"It's not Ruby," she managed.

She tottered to her feet and threw herself against David.

"It's not Ruby." She couldn't stop saying, "It's not Ruby." Today, someone else would have to suffer the loss. Not her, not yet. "It's not Ruby."

They walked toward the body. The sheriff gestured for Kate to stay away.

"What do you think, David?"

The doctor bent down. He delicately touched the bones in the face and glanced at the reconstructive surgery in the pubic area. She hadn't been dead long.

"Drowned probably," he said.

"By herself?" the sheriff puzzled, pointing across the meadow to the spot that marked the center of the plush green hollow. "Over there?"

"The blow to her face was hard but probably not fatal. My educated guess is it knocked her out. Maybe she was drunk or stoned, fell down, injured herself, got up, fell in, unable to lift her head. Or she was punched and pushed."

"Assuming it was foul play, why drag her over here?"

"Less of a chance of finding her in a grave."

"Are you sure she drowned?"

"Not positive," David said. He picked a few tiny sprigs from Charlene's blond hair. "Villagers come here to get watercress."

Sheriff, inspector, evidence team, and doctor made a sweep of a large circumference around the pond. Two bottles of champagne, a crushed box of crackers, a bloody bandanna were recovered. There was also a footprint in the mud by the pond.

Kate sat beneath a juniper. She had been taken into the pit, singed by hellfire, shown a hole nothing could fill. And then spared. By that miracle alone, she'd been given a second chance. She had been given the right to live again.

"What do you make of it, doctor?"

"No idea," David said weakly.

Information on the license plate confirmed it was not a rental car but a private vehicle registered to Robert Russo, resident of Tesuque. Russo didn't know the current whereabouts of the car although he confirmed his cousin, Charlene Russo, had borrowed it for a weekend trip with a friend. He hadn't heard from her since she left. He knew nothing about her companion, neither name nor gender. He had no reason to report either Charlene or the car missing. He refused to answer questions about Charlene's sexual identity or questions about the company she generally kept. He tearfully mentioned she had moved to Santa Fe to take care of him because he was sick. He was so sick he could barely walk. The inspector had to wheel him into the morgue in Santa Fe to view the corpse. Identification positive.

A trace turned up Russo's car in a parking lot on Second Street in downtown Albuquerque. Within walking distance of both train and bus stations. An officer was dispatched with a photo of Ruby Ryan to nearby restaurants, shops, hotels. The car was held as evidence for murder, assault, and kidnapping. A policeman was posted on the floor of the hospital where Tory Mason had been admitted.

David and Kate returned to the Ryan place. The police and sheriff deputies had left, the villagers gone home. They were alone.

"If Ruby ran away, where would she go?" David asked.

"If she had money?"

"Money for a bus, train, plane, where would she go?"

Kate disappeared into Ruby's inner sanctum. She lifted a floorboard where Ruby kept her valuables: money, a silver ID bracelet that belonged to her father, a locket Kate gave her, a cameo of Kate's mother.

"Did you find something?" David asked.

"Her cash and her dad's bracelet are missing."

"Forget kidnappers. Take away Troy, the corpse, August, the car. Where would Ruby go?"

A filament of hope flickered in Kate's brain. She wrote out the names and phone numbers of her sister in New Haven, Ruby's best friend in Tucson, and Marnie Ryan, Edwin's first cousin.

David made three uncomfortable phone calls. He explained that Ruby was missing. Telegraphing the word *missing* to each coast underscored the magnitude of the problem. Ruby could be anywhere.

They both jumped when David's mobile rang.

"Dr. Tanner," a voice crackled over the line. "This is Marnie Ryan, Kate's cousin. I got your message about Ruby."

"Marnie, is she there?" He turned over the phone receiver so Kate could listen too.

"She isn't here but you should know that Quinn is at the old place in Idaho. He's spending the summer there."

"That's *exactly* where Ruby would go," Kate's heart quickened.

"Can you give us the number in Idaho?"

"There's no phone but I have a number for the grocer. I'll call him. He might be willing to drive over to the house. He knew the kids when they were little. He might be willing to help."

26

At four in the morning, Troy hobbled past the guard through the receiving doors of Saint Vincent's Hospital. He had a crutch, a bottle of painkillers, his wallet, Edwin Ryan's checkbook, a wad of money, and his comatose roommate's clothes. Mobility was painful but in a few minutes, he reached the center of town. The Plaza looked like a discarded stage set, empty, gray, but fancifully picturesque. No one was out or about. A single cab sat outside the La Fonda Hotel. Troy knocked at the window and offered the driver two hundred dollars to drive him south.

For the first fifteen miles, he lay on the taxi's backseat. Every mile that distanced him from Santa Fe and the law was a fluke, an answered prayer. If Charlene's head flared in the car window, he replaced it with a picture of Ruby Ryan. Ruby, he could hate, no problem. But Charlene tugged on him in a different way. She'd soon be missed, then found. Somebody bright might connect the dots, especially if Ruby was available to testify about Charlene's cousin's car. Ruby's word could send him to prison for life.

The highway dipped into the Rio Grande valley where the city spread in all directions, west across the river and mesas and east to the Sandias, the mountains that at sunset glow as pink as watermelon, their namesake. Troy got out at The Antler on Central Avenue, an easy place to sit unnoticed. What he liked about The Antler was what everyone liked. It never changed. Year after year, even the waitresses were the same. Hitchhiking between Texas and California had taken him there on numerous occasions. Although The Antler boasted many amenities for travelers, especially truckers, its greatest attraction was the best pie between Amarillo and Flagstaff.

Troy chose a booth under a velvet painting of a 1960 red Impala convertible, his all-time favorite ride. He removed everything from his bulky wallet: business cards, fake IDs, glossy photos of Christie Brinkley's kids, receipts.

Among the chits was the name and phone number of an Albuquerque resident, a young man he befriended in a dust storm near Bakersfield. For thirteen hours, they were stranded in a parking lot in the middle of Nowhere, California. The dust storm was fierce, zero visibility, freeway traffic stopped. Every car had paint damage and pockmarks on its glass. Once the ordeal of waiting was over, the man's car wouldn't start. Sand in the carburetor, Troy diagnosed, and fixed it. Dom made him promise if there was ever anything *he* could do, Troy would call.

"I hope this is good," Dom coughed sleepily into the receiver.

"Dominic, it's Edwin Ryan, remember me?" As soon as Troy lied, he felt a surge of warmth. *White lies*, his mother called them. Like stories, they vanished into air. "I hope I didn't wake you."

"Edwin who?"

"I fixed your car outside Bakersfield last year."

"You saved my bass-ackward, man! It was the biggest favor anyone ever did for me in my entire life! But your name wasn't Edwin, was it?"

"Did you call me 'Troy'?"

"Yeah," Dom said.

"Some friends call me Edwin, others Troy, goose bird, asshole, et cetera," he chuckled. "I answer to all of the above."

"Hope you aren't stranded in Bakersfield?"

"I'm in your neighborhood. But I had a bad accident. I busted my knee. I lost my Land Rover. I'm a little disoriented from pain and pain-killers. I know it's early but I could really use a hand if you're not busy."

"I'm there, man," Dom said.

Troy suggested breakfast at The Antler.

After handshakes and hugs, Dom read the breakfast specials.

"I'm a vegan, man," he said.

Troy had forgotten what that was.

"I don't eat meat or cheese or milk or eggs. I don't wear leather. It's about man abusing and killing animals. I'm against that."

"That's good." Troy smiled across the table. "Good to have strong beliefs. But if man doesn't kill animals, he'd probably kill a whole lot more men."

Dom's eyebrows knit together in a unibrow. "If man doesn't kill animals, he'd kill more men," he repeated thoughtfully.

Despite the pain and fatigue, Troy's blue eyes twinkled with charm.

"I'm contemplating here what's most important on the food chain. Man or pig?"

"About the same," Dom declared.

"If I was you, I'd think again."

Dom ate his fruit salad and English muffin while Troy devoured eggs, biscuits, bacon, and pancakes.

"That was pleasant," Troy said. "You know, hunger is a terrible thing. They say a man is only nine meals away from murder."

"A cannibal?"

"No, I mean your ordinary guy who's hungry enough to kill anything. Hungriest I ever been was lost on a patrol in Iraq for two days. That was almost nine meals."

They leaned back in the booth under the airbrushed Impala.

"Thank you, Mr. Ryan," Dom said.

"I was lucky you were home. This was supposed to be my vacation," Troy snorted. "Trying to get out of those goddamn Blood of Christ mountains, I had a freak accident with my shotgun. Bam! Had to wait three hours for an ambulance to find me. They fixed me up at the hospital and I hitched a taxi ride here." He rubbed his bandaged knee. "Hurts like a son-of-a-bitch!"

"I bet it does."

"I can't hunt. I can't hike. I guess the next best thing is a beautiful fishing spot where I can recuperate. My dilemma is having to decide what beautiful spot to pick. You ever have that problem?"

With two jobs and courses at the community college, Dom hadn't relaxed in months.

"Where would *you* lie around?" Troy asked him.

Dom was flattered. His opinion rarely mattered about anything.

"Hawaii, no brainer."

"You got that right. I used to spend lots of time in Maui. You been to Maui? You can walk into the center of the volcano. But no way my knee is going on an airplane, even first class. I couldn't make it from here to San Diego."

"That's cold, man," Dom said.

"I'm not giving up on my vacation. I hear great things about Idaho. Fishing in Idaho sound good to you?"

"I went there once with my pop."

"I believe you mentioned that in Bakersfield. You said it was the last time you and your dad . . . ? Before he . . . ?"

"Yeah, pop and me caught some real beauties," Dom choked up. "After that was when they found the cancer."

"Good memories left in Idaho," Troy said.

"It isn't far by plane," Dom suggested.

"Car's better. I can stop and stretch. I can lie down in the backseat."

"I guess you don't want to be cooped up."

Troy regarded the young man's carefully brushed hair, his clean shirt, his stonewashed jeans, his white leather sneakers.

"It would be unbearable," Troy said. "That's why I need a driver. You know a kid with a car who wants to take a vacation? All expenses paid?"

"I wish I could help," Dom said with longing. "It feels like I *almost* won the lottery."

"You ever hear the expression, *carpus diem*? It's more than an expression, it's a philosophy of life." Troy stared into Dom's trusting hazelnut eyes. "I turned chances down myself. But then, I decided to seize the day. That's what *carpus diem* means in Roman." He inserted quickly, "Maybe you can say a good friend in Idaho got hurt? And you have to go up there and nurse him for a week or so?"

Dom's eyebrows drew together in a dark hairy line.

"I can see lying disturbs you. That shows you're trustworthy. But I'm not asking you to lie. I wouldn't do that." Troy ticked off the perks. "I pay gas, meals, motels. There won't be camping. Plus a cash bonus." Troy's final appeal. "Isn't it almost as bad as killing a cow to refuse an old friend in time of need?"

27

During the afternoon, frightened people streamed into the clinic, asking questions Elaine couldn't answer. Now the man with the answers had returned.

"David," she hyperventilated. "Did you see the body?" Suddenly, she burst into hot angry tears.

"It wasn't Ruby," he said.

"What?" Elaine sputtered, her grief wasted.

"It's not Ruby," he repeated coldly. He wanted to avoid the fetid details. Above all, he wanted to sleep.

He reeled into his office and locked the door. At the window was the panorama of sky and mountains. The weatherbeaten beauty only exacerbated the disaster. He touched his pulse, his hair, his familiar and unfamiliar face, his self, stranger and friend, and collapsed on his cot, trying to blot out the broken and carelessly buried body. He felt for the loose floorboard, lifted and removed a safe box. Holding the box steady, he opened his treasure chest. Inside were vials of Fentanyl and Buprenex, a bindle of high-grade heroin, an envelope of crystal meth, Fentanyl candies, opium suppositories, Thai sticks, baggies of Mexican pot, an old cache of windowpane acid, and ampules of codeine. Variations of whatever it took to let him dream the dreams of a happy man.

He swabbed the web of skin between his largest toes with alcohol. The brilliant moon-cold sensation and smell sent a thrill through him, his psychic engine preparing for takeoff. He had a great affection for his weakness. Weakness was human. Weakness is what separated humans from gods, although in some mythologies it was precisely what connected them.

He stuck the tip of the needle between his toes and waited to see blood. Then, he connected the syringe to the tail of the butterfly needle and sank the plunger. Removing the needle, he pushed the works under his pillow, leaned back, inhaled, and waited. He began to float. Up, he floated. Or down, he couldn't tell. He passed a dozen floors en route to oblivion, each with snapshots of memory: his wedding photo, his high school gym teacher, a playground swing, Judy Moskowitz's nipples. Judy Moskowitz? He giggled. And always the river, the constant that led to the confluence of many rivers. Rivers of the west where he'd rafted and rowed past golden forests and tiger-striped cliffs. Mountain rivers, desert rivers, ribbons of water, flat and foaming. The double life of Dr. Tanner had trained him in the art of prestidigitation. When he reached his final destination, he would disappear. Evening checkout, morning return.

At dawn, he awoke. He left his office and headed a mile north to his low rambling adobe that sat solid like earth, made of earth, welcoming him. A sack lay by the door, a note tucked under the knocker. He fondled the paper in Kate's careful handwriting—

Chopped mint and ground ivy soothe sleep, prevent nightmares.
Love, K

He pushed on the unlocked door into the old adobe. White plastered walls, *viga* beams across the ceilings, tiled fireplaces, earthen floors polished with ox blood, and a profusion of woven and leather pillows. He put his dirty dishes in the sink to soak. He tidied his reading materials. He transported dirty clothes to the washing machine in the back shed. He stripped the two beds and changed the towels. While coffee brewed, he selected *Madame Butterfly*. Puccini was not his favorite composer. He preferred Donizetti and Verdi, but Puccini was dependably pleasing.

Most important, it was *Madame Butterfly* that he and Kate had heard in Santa Fe. A stark production that referenced apocalyptic Hiroshima in August 1945 with Butterfly played by a Japanese soprano, Pinkerton by an Italian, both handsome with strong acting abilities. Throughout the performance, David felt Kate's unwavering attention on Butterfly, the abandoned woman. She wept without embarrassment. At dinner, she wept again.

David was back at the clinic by nine where there was a message from Marnie Bass to call her.

"Any news?" she asked.

"We had a bad scare yesterday," David said. "A young woman's body was found in the forest. It's likely she was murdered."

Marnie gasped.

"The fear is Ruby will be discovered next."

"I wish I could tell you she's in Idaho."

"But?"

"I'm not sure," Marnie said. "I called the grocer in Salmon. Quinn recently came in and bought two or three cartons of canned food. That's a lot for a boy who favors fresh vegetables."

"What do you think it means?"

"Maybe he's going out on the river but hasn't told me. Then again, he might not. He knows I'm a worrier. Even if you know what you're doing and Quinn doesn't, it's dangerous. But if he were trying to hide?"

"Hide?"

"The grocer said he saw a girl walk off with Quinn. I asked if he remembered our cousin, Ruby. He wasn't sure. But he said he'd stop at the house."

David found Kate in her yard. She hadn't slept. She'd prayed all night.

"I spoke to Marnie," he said, taking her hand. "She called."

Kate started. "She spoke to Quinn?"

"She reached the grocer who's seen Quinn."

"Was he with someone?" Kate gripped David's hand.

"A girl was outside the store but he didn't see her face."

Kate threw her arms around David's neck. "That's her!"

"No, Kate!" He had to be realistic. He had to suppress her wild speculations. He was pessimistic by nature. Medical training made him risk-averse. And river life? The river was where David had found the line between competency and helplessness, control and surrender.

Kate pointed to the Dodge. "It can easily get to Idaho."

"Quinn probably has a girlfriend and doesn't want his mother to know."

"It's Ruby."

"But how could she get to Idaho?"

"I don't know but that's where she went. Quinn is Ruby's big brother. He'd be the one to help her."

"What if the police need you here?"

Kate shrugged. There was nothing more to discuss. Idaho was a long way. The drive would take close to twenty-four hours. It was a journey she knew well. She and Ruby had traveled there many summers to visit Ryan kin.

"What am I supposed to do?" David asked.

"Come with me," Kate begged. "Come help me find Ruby."

28

ugust leaned against the dusty Power Wagon, his eyes scanning the house. "I guess everyone's on edge, waiting for more bad news. They thought the worst about that girl. They thought it was Ruby but Ruby's too smart."

"Plenty of smart people get in trouble," Kate said.

"Maybe you think it's my fault," he blurted.

"Why would I?"

"The police think it."

"They don't know what they think," Kate sneered. "Troy walked out of the hospital past the guard."

"That sucks," August said. "Are *you* going somewhere?"

"I don't know," Kate hedged.

"It looks like you're going camping." He lifted a tarp from the ground. "If someone around here has to die, it should be me. Anyone but Ruby."

"You have to leave now, August. This isn't your business. This is *our* family's business." Kate gestured to the car. "If you tell anyone what you saw, I'll be forced to go to the police and say you brought drugs into my house."

"They weren't mine."

"Don't try to deny it!"

Abandonment swept through August. He'd known Kate Ryan since he was a little boy. She'd never once been cruel. She'd treated him with acceptance and affection. Now it seemed she didn't like him at all.

The front door to the clinic was ajar. Elaine sat behind the reception desk, a small fan blowing on her face.

"Is Dr. Tanner here?" August asked.

Elaine didn't smile or offer one of her cordial greetings. Instead, she pointed to his office. He took Elaine's unfriendliness as another personal affront. The whole world had turned on him.

"Can I come in, Dr. Tanner?"

A large satchel lay open on the doctor's cot. David stood, thumbing through river maps and guidebooks.

"Yes?" He sounded annoyed.

August sighed volubly. "I'm wondering if you can give me something to sleep. I feel sick. I feel sick all the time. I think I'm going crazy. Do you think that's possible? Of course, it's possible. But is it happening to me? My mother wants to take me to a psychiatrist because all I do is worry about Ruby. Maybe she's in trouble and I can't do anything because I don't know."

"It's a difficult time," David comforted him.

August thrust his face in his hands. "It's my fault," he cried.

"We all feel at fault here," he said.

"Can you give me a drug?" August finally managed.

"Elaine," David shouted through the door.

"What?" she shouted back angrily.

"Get August an envelope of Xanax, will you?"

Elaine studied her watch. It was past her official work time. She hadn't had a break in six hours or a vacation in eighteen months. Now the director of the clinic and the only board-certified doctor within miles was leaving on a wacko mission with a woman of unsound judgment. He'd asked Elaine to tell the police that an urgent family matter required his immediate attention. From her point of view, he'd compromised her and jeopardized the clinic.

David's packing was almost finished. He took his pillow off the cot and his poncho from a hook behind the door. He stuffed everything into the canvas satchel.

At home he stood on his patch of yard, scattered with cactus and juniper. He drenched his two pots of roses. Across the valley, dark streaks of rain sifted from the clouds like gunpowder, stopping in midsky and never reaching the ground. He studied the *virgas* evaporating in air and a feeling of lost happiness oscillated inside him.

Behind him rumbled Kate's car. She stopped, leaned over, smiled bravely. "Are you sure?" She was giving him a last chance to reconsider.

David's reserve receded. His eyes opened so that Kate could peer inside them, seeing him entirely. He closed the door, and Kate swung the car around, back to the highway, and headed to Idaho.

PART 2

29

Quintin Edwin Bass was Marnie's baby, named for her cousin, Edwin Ryan, who was killed by "friendly fire" during the last days of the Gulf War. His death precipitated the family's decision to move out of Oakland, away from the home wars of gangs and crime to a ramshackle house in Idaho that Marnie's husband had inherited. They would go there. Accustomed as they were to the mores of the Bay Area, they believed "folks were folks," meaning they were hopeful as they packed up their household and set out. The adjustment was difficult, especially for the three children. Only after a swastika appeared on their mailbox did the community rally. Sunday sermons were delivered, the town council passed a proclamation of tolerance, and the schools held special assemblies. Marnie and Ian became a welcome sight. They made good friends. Marnie was elected to the school board.

Shortly after they arrived in Salmon, Marnie received a letter from a woman who called herself Edwin's wife. She described their brief romance, the rash decision to marry, and later after Edwin left for Iraq, the discovery she was pregnant. She now lived in a village in northern New Mexico with Ruby Rosen Ryan, Edwin's daughter.

Kate wrote, *I want Ruby to know her father's family.*

"If Edwin was married, he'd have let us know," Marnie told her husband. "He would have brought her home, white or any color. It wouldn't have been a problem. They were already used to you."

Marnie wrote back, *Come visit us anytime.*

A couple of months later, Kate appeared in a battered Datsun station wagon with a playpen in the rear of the vehicle, a string of diapers hung to dry around a makeshift roof-rack, and chubby island-brown Ruby. When Marnie saw them, her doubts fell away. Ruby looked exactly like Edwin.

For several summers, Kate and Ruby visited the Bass family in their large accommodating clapboard house, part Victorian and part improvisation with a spacious kitchen, two small bedrooms, a parlor downstairs, and a roomy attic with bunk beds that served as a dormitory for the children. A screened porch wrapped around the sides of the house where eating and socializing took place, weather permitting.

When Quinn was eleven, they moved back to California. Marnie tried to keep the house in Salmon rented out but there had been no occupants in a year. At the end of his first year of college, Quinn headed to Idaho to fix the roof, replace the broken windows, paint the interior, and clear the overgrown yard.

Half asleep, he lay on the porch's daybed, inhaling honeysuckle and fresh-mown grass, daydreaming.

"What the hell!" he jumped.

Beside him was a spooky version of Ruby, older, taller, hollow-eyed with a cap of fuzz for hair. She'd traveled forty hours from Albuquerque to Twin Falls, changing buses in Denver and Salt Lake.

"Ruby?" he whispered.

"Quinn, it's me."

30

Breakfast was pannkakor, Marnie's specialty pancake. As kids, Quinn and Ruby used to compete over who could eat the most. Ruby always had something to prove. She wanted to outrun, outeat, and outwit her older cousin, Quinn. Now that he was in college, there was no contest. He was way ahead of her.

"I found the river stuff," he said. "In the garage where Dad left it. Raft, oars, rubber bags, ammo boxes, almost everything."

"Let's go!" she cried.

"If Dad was here, no problem," he said.

"*That* was my escape plan," Ruby confessed. To vanish down a water-hole to nowhere and never be found.

"I thought escaping Zamora was your escape plan."

"It won't take long for them to find me here."

"But you told your mom?"

"She wasn't home when I left. I'm afraid to tell her now."

"Kate is going to worry to death until you tell her."

"The police are watching her now. They want to know if I've made contact."

"What's that mean?"

"I had to leave, Quinn. I didn't have a choice."

Tears welled in Ruby's eyes.

"I shot a guy," she said.

"You joking?"

"It was an accident but I think I killed him."

"Like in self-defense?"

Quinn knew people who'd been shot, gunned down in the city. His cousin, Tommie, had died on the street. Marie, another cousin, was paralyzed from crossfire.

"He was coming after me."

"That's *not* murder," Quinn said.

"After I shot him, I took his car. I went to my friend's house. His mom came to the door. She told me August wasn't home. She told me to get away. I wish I hadn't told her anything. She's a bitch, his mom. I wish I hadn't left him a note. Whatever I said, she'll use against me. I'll go to jail for the rest of my life."

"It should be okay," Quinn said. "It was an accident. He was coming after you."

"They put kids in jail for way less than what I did. I need to hide."

"You're here. You're hiding."

"They'll say I shot him in cold blood."

"It was self-defense."

"I need to go on the river, Quinn. All the times your dad let you paddle, you can manage. If you won't take me, I'll go by myself."

Quinn slipped down the bank and waded into shallow water. He shoved the loaded raft with Ruby into the Main Fork of the Salmon and holding the tow line, sprang over the side of the boat, mounted a seat at the stern, and lifted the wooden oars lodged in the oar-locks. As the raft began to edge toward the fast central current, it was clear that Quinn had to take control or they would succumb to the river: its currents and subcurrents, its cascades and rapids rolling toward the Salmon's confluence with the Snake and Columbia and on to the Pacific. Rolling with powers measured in tens of thousands of cubic feet per second of water flow. Or by the height of its banks, the depth of its chasms, the inches of its descent, the tonnage of rocks crushed from boulder to sand. Or meted in the days it takes to row across the panhandle of Idaho. Or its mysterious sobriquet, River of No Return.

Quinn fumbled and the oars flapped until he found the syncopated motion forward back, forward back. He lifted and swung each oar in opposite directions, grinning happily. He had the hang of it. A feeling swelled in his body as if it were human instinct to navigate water in rafts, logs, canoes, barges, and boats. Back and forth, he rowed.

"You scared?" he shouted over the din of the river.

Ruby perched precariously on the forward thwart. Strapped behind her between the rowing platform and aft thwart were the black rubber, cube-shaped waterproof bags and watertight metal boxes filled with supplies. She shut her eyes and clutched the loops of hoopie that crisscrossed the raft. For the first time in days, she was overwhelmed by forces more frightening than crime and punishment. It was the dualistic force of water itself, the combination of yielding and forging, crushing and forgiving, moving inexorably toward its destination. However, as the rocking motion became familiar, her fingers unwound. Her eyes opened to the majesty of mountains, sky, and great trees along the shore. She smiled at Quinn with relief. They were launched.

A raft is required to have a permit on its bowline. It's required to register its length of stay and the names of its passengers. It's required to carry life jackets, a first-aid kit, a portable potty, extra oars, and paddles. The permits are issued in advance through a lottery system and regulate boat traffic on the Salmon.

With limited resources, Quinn had cobbled together the best equipment he could. The life jackets were top quality but the extra oar was a foot shorter than the match set. He used Ruby's money to buy food, a water filter, a dozen carabineers, and two second-hand sleeping bags. His father's old pump, rubber patch kit, World War II rocket and ammo boxes, bailing buckets, tent, and U.S. Geological Survey maps that described the Main rapid-by-rapid and mile-by-mile were still serviceable. Rain gear and woolen sweaters they purchased at a thrift store. The portable potty was improvised with a bucket and sealed lid. It was too late to secure a genuine permit so Quinn forged one and tied it to the bowline. He gathered supplies, chatted with professional guides about Class III rapids, and practiced rowing techniques in the river's eddies.

When a special-delivery letter arrived from Marnie, he announced, "We're going in the morning."

Ruby's resolve weakened. Raft, river, the two of them, it had the ring of disaster.

"The police are searching for you. A girl's body was found in Zamora."

"They think I'm dead?"

"Kidnapped or dead," Quinn said.

Their eyes locked. Their futures were bound together, written in the blood of Ruby's father and Quinn's mother, the blood of ancestors transported as slaves from West Africa to Louisiana and their great-grandparents who migrated from Louisiana to California. Their lives were in each other's keeping.

31

The Salmon is one of the longest undammed rivers in the west. After heavy winter storms and spring thaws, volumes of water and debris flow down. As a result, the river changes, providing wild beauty and sport even for those who know it well.

For almost an hour, the rubber raft bounced through chop, the run long and safe enough for Quinn to find his rhythm and Ruby to overcome her anxiety. At the ranger station at Corn Creek, there were several rafting parties sorting and loading. River guides and passengers waved as they floated by. No rangers in sight.

They heard their first roar of white water eight miles south of Corn Creek. A sound that made them want to leap ashore. Ruby turned to Quinn for reassurance but his eyes were fixed on a narrow horizon that had dropped and vanished. Within seconds, they were sucked into the crashing current.

"Hold on!" he shouted.

Ruby seized a web of hoopie and braced herself.

Quinn's limited task was to keep the craft from drifting out of center. Using the bow as rudder, he aimed into the tower of waves and gripped the oars. White water crashed over them, boulders rose on either side but without mishap, they shot through Rainier rapid into a serene green pool.

The roaring water was behind them. Only luck and the forgiving force of river had brought them safely through. Quinn had no illusions. He brooded how he'd manage the challenges of Devil's Teeth, Salmon Falls, and Big Mallard.

"Your turn," he smiled from his captain's post, tossing Ruby the bailing bucket.

A mile farther, they saw an empty camp. Quinn angled the oars to maneuver them into an eddy, then rowed upstream to the beach. Two logs, a fire pit, and willows made a cooking area. A rock overhang provided shelter in case of rain. A bank of scree sloped up to a Douglas fir for privacy.

"Home," he sighed as childhood feelings of playing house with Ruby Ryan rushed through him.

They pitched camp and watched parties of rafts, kayaks, and dories drift by to campsites farther downstream. Ruby marveled at the flat-bottom, colorful wooden dories, popular for river travel since the nineteenth century. Although less maneuverable and dull by comparison, the rafts were serviceable and dependable, hand-powered with paddles or oars. The only reminder of combustion engines were the noisy jetboats downshifting, bouncing over rapids, leaving trails of exhaust behind.

The clear river and pristine white sand, the forests on the sides of the mountains, the high ridges aflame at sunrise and sunset, the place belonged to Quinn's father. It was the gift of place that his father and grandfather had passed down to him.

Upstream, a moose cow and calf dipped their heads into the river. The giant mother sashayed through the water and crossed to the other bank while the calf tottered on shore, watching her go and return. The mother repeated the exercise but the calf held back. When Quinn honked a poor imitation of a moose call, the cow turned toward the sound, then indifferently led her calf away.

"You ass!" Ruby said, their laughter exploding between the canyon walls.

They tumbled across the sand and slipped into the puddle-warm water at the shoreline. Ruby unpacked tuna, baked beans, green apples, bread. If they ate sparingly, their food would last a month. In their sleeping bags under a carpet of stars, she groped for Quinn's hand.

"Eternity and infinity have affinity," she said.

"Right," he muttered, already asleep.

32

David and Kate drove, slept, drove, and slept in three-hour shifts, stopping only for gas and food. They reached Salmon the next night.

"Ruby!" Kate bounded up the steps of the old porch. "Ruby! Quinn!" she cried, reaching for the key hidden under a brick.

David followed her into the empty kitchen, empty hall, empty parlor, empty attic, empty garage.

"They're not here," she admitted.

"*He* is not here," David said.

She circled the kitchen and combed the rooms again. The night air was warm, redolent with the lingering smells of a hot day.

"He signed Marnie's letter two days ago. He was here then."

"True," David said, noncommittal.

"Maybe they took off to San Francisco."

"Maybe they did. But now, you and I are going to sleep. Doctor's orders."

Kate started to speak.

"Shush," he said.

Kate glanced at his back as he turned and removed his shirt and jeans. He wasn't her typical drifter. Not pretty or lean or boyish. He was a man, she thought. Maybe someone who had come to terms with himself.

"Tell me a story." She sounded like Ruby.

"A tale?"

"A story about you."

"Once," he began. Maybe he could talk them both to sleep. Kate sank, letting the softness take her away. "I was on a river. I was thin and young and brown with lots of hair," he laughed. "A Paiute in a canoe, paddling through geologic time. Locked inside the strata of the canyons, each eon rose from past to present. I could read the eons in the rock. A man in a boat on a river, moving forward in space and backward in time from Paiute to Anasazi to the tribes whose names we don't know."

She folded into his body, drifting on the river of sleep.
"I used to be a visitor in my own life," he said.
"Go on," she murmured.
"But on the river, I finally felt a part."

33

As Dom drove north, Troy settled into a new arrangement of events. There were three, maybe four primary players which he pushed around, changing their relationships until he and Charlene were almost totally separated. An acquaintanceship, a couple of favors, a few beers at Jackson's, that was the extent of Charlene Russo. His mission was to find the girl who shot him, killed Charlene, and stole her car. That would be Ruby Ryan. The story was working but the painkillers made him drowsy. Each time he woke, there was another puzzle in his reconstituted past.

He asked Dom, "You ever heard of *pressed* memories?"

"*Re*-pressed," Dom said.

"Know what it means?"

The young man chewed thoughtfully on a banana chip. As company, Dom had started to wear thin. In Troy's opinion, he fell into a category of men who talked too much about things no one wanted to hear and when asked a direct question, refused to open his mouth. However, Dom couldn't be rushed. He waited until the chip had been thoroughly masticated before he spoke.

"After a bad thing happens, sometimes it's so bad you don't remember. Maybe your mind chooses not to remember. You *repress* it. You with me?"

"Copy," Troy said.

"It's like a pancake in your brain. When you *repress*, it gets flatter and flatter and sinks to the bottom of all your other memories. Then, it disappears. It happens all the time. That's why they call it a 'syndrome.'"

"Syndrome," Troy mumbled. "I got a case of that syndrome."

"You probably heard about daddies and daughters? The worst part, I mean the second worst part is they can't remember daddy doing anything bad."

"Kids forget all kinds of things," Troy said. "What about adults who can't remember?"

"Like amnesia?"

"Let's say, a grown-up puts something out of his mind. Right now, I got a bad feeling but I can't wrap myself around it. It's at the end of a tunnel. I try to reach out to touch it but I'm scared shitless. Something like that?"

Dom's eyes moistened with concern.

"Sound like one of those syndrome things?"

"Did it happen a long time ago?"

"It just happened."

"My buddy who went to Iraq, he's doing EMDR for PTSD."

"Too many initials," Troy said.

"But everything is coming back to him. It's working."

"This is right before I took it in the knee."

"Your hunting accident?"

"I have a feeling I forgot the most important part." Troy clutched his stomach. "Can you stop the car?"

Dom pulled into a rest area. Troy lifted himself out and hobbled on a crutch a few yards away.

"Better," he shouted, limping back to the car. "The mind is strange. Suddenly, she was there."

"Like who?"

"She wanted to go hunting with me. My mistake but she was pretty. Half-breed of something."

"The prettiest," Dom agreed.

Troy's voice grew low as he recalled. "We drove north of Santa Fe to Zamora. You know Zamora up in those Blood of Christ mountains? I stopped to see my friend. She wasn't home, but her teenage daughter asked if she could come with us. She likes guns."

"It's all inside the tunnel," Dom coached. "Keep going, you'll get there."

"I think we stopped for a hitchhiker."

"Hitchhikers are trouble," Dom said. "My cousin was tortured by a hitchhiker."

"This hitchhiker? Maybe he did something bad to the women. Maybe my friend's daughter did something bad. All I know is I'm shot."

"That's a lot of recovery."

"I should talk to the police," Troy cried out. "They might need me to identify something."

Dom mustered every shred of reasoning available to him. "It doesn't make sense to go to police in Utah for something that *maybe* happened in New Mexico. But I can take us back to Albuquerque if you want."

"I sound like a nut case." Troy said, slapping his good knee.

"Especially since you can't say what it is that happened."

"You convinced me, buddy. I'm putting this foggy tunnel aside and going fishing."

"Let your mind relax," Dom touched Troy's belly.

"You ain't queer, are you?"

"Relax," Dom said. "If you exhale from your navel, things will get clearer."

Outside Salt Lake, Troy insisted on a deluxe motel. The next day, refreshed and well-fed, they drove through beautiful high desert country, irrigated farms, tidy Mormon towns, dry red mounds of rock that stretched in the distance to dry red mountains. Troy was in a good mood. Things were falling into place.

In Twin Falls, while Dom telephoned his girlfriend, Troy went sightseeing at the local gun shop. He picked up a spiffy S&W double action .38 special. From Twin Falls, he pointed Dom north, as if his hand were on a tiller, meandering though Sun Valley and continuing on back roads across the valleys of the Sawtooth Mountains. North to the little town of Salmon, a dot on the map that Ruby and Kate used to discuss. The place Ruby held up as a refuge from Zamora. Details that Troy remembered with a kind of genius.

"I got a friend in Salmon," he said. "Somebody I helped out at a rest stop in Oregon. Paul told me to come visit if I was ever in the neighborhood. At the time, I didn't think that was likely, but you never know, do you?"

"Seems like you helped out people all over the place," Dom said.

34

They stayed an extra day on the beach. When other rafters stopped to picnic, Quinn plied the guides with the same questions. As for Salmon Falls, the guides agreed the greatest danger was the suck hole.

"Keep to the middle and row like a son-of-a-bitch," they said.

Ruby wanted to stay where they were although it wasn't prudent. Upstream, the boat traffic was concentrated. Downstream, everyone dispersed, traveling at different speeds. It was better to be downstream.

"No pictures of Missing Persons," Quinn reminded her. "And no rangers."

Once they heard the roar of Salmon Falls, Quinn veered right, grabbed an eddy, and moored the raft to a tree. They scurried up the embankment to the scouting point. At the top of the cliff overlooking the river, their legs crumbled. Shouting over the din, Quinn pointed to the narrow passage between two suctioning whirlpools and a foaming hole.

"What do you think?" Ruby asked.

"I can't *think*," Quinn said.

They stayed at the observation point, delaying the run through the great white tumble until other rafts passed by. From upriver, a jetboat raced along. At the edge of the drop-off, it downshifted and bumped over the tumult of rock, hole, and water. Once the rough ride was over, passengers turned back to view the cascading river. As the jetboat shoved its throttle into high gear and sped off, Ruby burst into tears.

"Don't worry," Quinn said, bowing his head to hide his fear and distress. "I'm going by myself. You'll walk the path and meet me at the pool."

"He's here!" she sobbed.

Quinn took Ruby's hand, wiped her tears, smoothed her hair. "Ruby, Ruby, he's not here."

"But I saw him!"

"Seriously, Ruby?"

"He's the only one who knew I was coming to Idaho."

Quinn was familiar with symptoms of paranoia and hallucinations. His uncle had a psychotic breakdown. Whenever his uncle went off his meds, he became delusional. Ruby probably needed psychological counseling, not a month in the wilderness.

"I saw the boat too," he said firmly. "There was a driver and six passengers. One of them looked like Troy, right?"

"Exactly like Troy."

"Blue shirt and straw hat, I bet that was the guy."

She nodded.

"He also looked like my high school chemistry teacher, Mr. Allen. It happens, Ruby. It happens all the time. Mistaken identity."

What Quinn said made sense. What Ruby saw made no sense. It was better to give into reason. The terrifying falls had probably set her off. Quinn reassured her until she believed him. Quinn had to be right. He was always right. There were no ghosts, no ghosts, no ghosts.

35

The grocery store in Salmon carried everything in a can or box plus fresh summer vegetables and fruit in bins on the sidewalk. Tom Bracken, the owner, was friendly, potbellied, and usually flushed with a pink-tinged face and bald head. When he spoke, he squinted to underscore his interest in whatever anyone had to say. He could recite quantity, brand, and cost of food that any recent customer bought, including Quinn Bass who'd purchased twelve small cans of chunky pineapple. Tom Bracken had the memory of an idiot savant. He also made enough money during tourist season to winter in Manzanillo, Mexico.

"When they moved over here from California, there was a stir. I thought we might have a riot in Salmon. Nobody ever seen an ebony-and-ivory family except on TV. A few dumb rednecks got excited. But if you asking me, I'd rather have a heap of decent coloreds than one piece of white scum. Nobody more decent than Marnie Bass."

"You remember when we used to visit?" Kate pulled out a photo of Ruby taken in seventh grade.

"Sure, I remember." He stared at the photo of a smiling child with lots of hair. The girl he saw with Quinn was grown up, curves and all. "Tall, I grant you that but black, Indian, Mexican, damn if I know. She stood on the sidewalk with a big hat while the Bass boy was in here buying out the store. He didn't answer when I asked where he was headed. 'Shopping for the end of the world?' I asked."

Besides groceries, Tom's official business was the business of everyone who entered Salmon. "I drove out to the Bass place after Marnie called. Didn't see boy or girl. Somebody in trouble?"

Tom pulled on his ear. If there was trouble, he wanted to be the first to know. He prided himself as town crier: first to know, first to tell. His store was a crossroads of information. He collected newspaper clippings of rafting mishaps, hunting accidents, lightning strikes, rodeo casualties, and bear and wildcat attacks. He himself was an attraction. If anyone in town was lonely or bored, they were welcome at Tom's store.

"I saw one of them amphibious assault crafts in the yard. Maybe a pump and a few beat-up rocket boxes. Check with the rangers at Corn Creek. If they're on the river, the rangers will know."

In the afternoon, Kate and David made the two-hour journey to Corn Creek, passing miles of potato and soybean fields until they reached the shady dirt road that paralleled the course of the river. To David's educated eye, the water was running high and fast.

"They wouldn't go out there alone," Kate said.

"Ruby already ran away. If the river was a way to keep running, she might take her chances."

"I know Quinn has more sense."

"Maybe, maybe not," David said. At Quinn's age, he and friends cut out after exams and drove from Berkeley to the Rogue. Ill-equipped and unprepared, reckless and unskilled, their first day on the river, David almost drowned. A friend broke a leg and had to be helicoptered out. They all came back sick with bronchitis and giardia.

"Do you think they're out there?" Kate asked.

David now believed what Kate believed. When they left Zamora, he thought she was in a dangerous state of mind. He came along to protect her from disappointment. Now he saw the logic of Ruby finding her way to Quinn. Kate trusted her instincts about Ruby. David trusted Kate. He guessed they'd come and gone although the rangers had no record. As for permits, cancellations meant there were a couple available onsite.

The river spoke to David. It awakened a liveliness in him. The Main Fork's technical rapids were not so difficult. He'd rafted the Salmon in the past.

"If they're on the river, we have to go," Kate said.

By the time they returned to town, they'd decided on a course of action. While David went to rent equipment, Kate returned to Tom Bracken's store with a list of supplies.

"Looks like you're going out on the River of No Return," Tom chuckled. "We enjoy calling it that, although some folks get spooked. Indians used to claim that no one who ventured downstream was ever seen again. At least, that's what Lewis and Clark heard. It's running fast but your husband won't have a problem. It sounds like he knows what he's doing. Maybe 19,000 CFS, maybe more. This time of year, it's usually eight thousand. We seen worse. They'll be a few accidents whether it's running high or low. That's what keeps life interesting."

He yammered as Kate zipped up and down the aisles.

"Your husband sounds like he knows what he's doing," Tom called out.

"He's not my husband," Kate said.

"I remember when you'd come to visit Quinn's mother."

"My husband was Marnie's first cousin."

"You drove from down south somewhere?"

"New Mexico," she said.

Tom recalled Ruby. She was a beautiful child.

"I forget your last name."

"Ryan," Kate said.

"I got a bunch of coincidences marching through this store on a daily basis. Folks discovering folks they haven't laid eyes on in twenty years wind up in this place for cosmic reasons. It's one of them *power spots* they talk about. This morning, a couple of guys was in here from New Mexico, name of Ryan."

Kate half-listened as she inventoried canned vegetables and fish, bags of nuts and dry fruit, cartons of eggs, packages of bread, bacon, pasta, and quarts of bottled water, soda, and beer.

"Sorry?" she turned to Tom.

"Ain't that something? Two Ryan gentlemen from New Mexico stopped in this morning."

"Odd," Kate said.

"Good-looking guy with lots of hair, one of those Clint Eastwood types. Asked if I knew where some colored people lived. That kind of question, I don't answer. I told him he had the wrong town. The fellow told me he had a friend who lived here name of Paul Jones. I told him I knew everybody. Never heard of Paul Jones. He went to write me a check for five bottles of tequila. Of course, we can't accept such things. It's a shame you can't trust nobody. When he put his checkbook on the counter, I saw his name, *Edwin Ryan* from New Mexico."

Kate stopped. "Edwin Ryan? You sure?"

"In a car with New Mexico plates. Kinda hobbled around."

"What do you mean 'hobbled'?"

"Said he'd been in a hunting accident. Going out on the river to relax and fish. Had a young man along to help him."

"Young man?"

"College kid who told me about this vegan craze. He follows it like a religion. He told me I could purify myself if I stopped eating enchiladas, pizza, ice cream. I asked how a man was supposed to live like that."

36

Ruby skirted the cliff to an outcrop of rocks where she could see Quinn clear the danger of the falls. Between the dome of sky and rushing flow, she waited. Above her, open and infinite. Below, unpredictable and savage.

Quinn rowed the raft from the safety of the eddy and entered the vortex of water. He looked confident and steady as he pulled. Every muscle strained against the current, pulling toward the ribbon that transected the hole and boulder. It appeared he would prevail but in an instant, the rushing water swept him to the right, sucked the raft to the edge of the hole, and flipped it. Quinn disappeared in the mouth of the rapid. The empty raft, upside down, bounced until it was lifted into the current and shot downstream.

When Quinn fell out of the raft, he knocked his head on rock. For a few seconds, he tumbled inside the whirlpool, battling the water. The harder he battled, the greater the struggle to find air. He expected to die in Salmon Falls.

As soon as Ruby saw him, she scrambled down the side of the cliff along the portage path, flung herself into the pool of flat water, and towed Quinn to the shore. He was dazed, bloody, speechless.

At the crest of the descent, four dories conducted a flawless waltz step toward the same narrow ribbon of water and passed without incident through Salmon Falls.

"Your raft gone?" an oarsman shouted, rowing over.

"Gone," Quinn said weakly.

"What about your head?"

Ruby pressed her bandana on Quinn's wound. "I guess it's okay," he said.

"Maybe the raft got hung up in an eddy," the guide said. "Come with us. We'll look for your stuff along the way."

37

Kate and David sat by the shore, the river's rhythms coursing inside them. It had been a glorious day on the water. Dinner was his river specialty, vegetable curry with rice and sautéed plantain. He cooked while Kate talked. The night was clear. They would forego the tent and sleep outside, lying on top of their inflatable pads, a sleeping sheet thrown over them.

He took Kate's hand and pressed it on his lips. "Okay?" he asked, rolling on top of her.

"Ruby," she whispered.

"We'll find Ruby," he said, rolling off.

For a few minutes, they looked at the velvet night sky, counting shooting stars.

"Penny for your thoughts?"

"One penny, one thought," he said.

"Like?" she laughed. David Tanner often made her laugh.

"Like what an orgasm is."

"*Is*?" she chortled, suspecting another attempt at foreplay.

"Laugh away!"

"Tell me, Dr. Orgasm."

"I'm serious."

"I can be serious."

"You've got nerves in special places?"

"Noted," she said.

"Stimulated by pressure, these nerves trigger or generate desires intended to propagate the species. I'd call that a standard definition, agreed?"

"Yes, doctor."

"But before we were born, before we were anything, there was an original neural feeling of father's sperm bombarding mother's ovum. When that happened, there was a big burst of . . ." he groped for the word.

"Excitement?" Kate suggested.

Laughter.

"Yes, atoms were filled with tremendous physical excitement and later when we had orgasms, it was *that* feeling our body remembered. The first sensation we ever had. What the French call *le petit mort*, but it's exactly opposite, *la petite vie*." His face broke open in a sheepish smile. "Interesting theory, huh?"

"Funny," she murmured as she drifted to sleep.

David reached for the origin of pleasure, semihard. With coaxing, it would respond. He watched Kate, her nipples beneath the thin cotton shirt and hair spread under her like a fan. He listened to her soft sleep-filled breaths. His eyes swiveled to the sky. He tried to restrain his heartbeat and the motion of his hand. But his hand acted of its own accord until he was hard, stiff, upright. He wanted to defer the pleasure, but against his will another will overtook him. And the oldest feeling inside him exploded.

38

The Lazy OK was an excellent hideaway. Comfortable accommodations, splendid views, bountiful breakfasts, venison and trout dinners, pleasant company. It was here that Troy planned to convalesce while Dom fished. After two days in the wilderness, his plans for vengeance had been whittled away, his fury and fears abated. If Ruby was in Idaho, so what? Let her rot. As for Charlene, she was a nightmare from a different man's past. Arrest warrants faded to remote possibility. The serenity of the Lazy OK prompted a saner plan: a layover until his knee healed, west by jetboat to Riggins followed by a ride to Boise, and after a change of names and forged passport, a visit to Canada.

In the afternoon, Troy sat by the porch railing, nursing his knee, contemplating the splendors of the river, feeling a measure of contentment and calm. He'd exchanged boots and jeans for shorts, sneakers, and Dom's purple polo shirt.

At the dock, a guide wrapped the line from his dory to a metal cleat. "Mr. Odegard around?" he shouted up to Troy.

Troy waved from his perch, frightened for a moment that authorities might be searching for him on the river. However, common sense prevailed. No law enforcement officer would arrive in a painted fairy boat.

Troy shambled down to the water where the four dories were docked.

"How y'all doing," he said, his tan rugged face, sun-streaked hair, and lanky body the epitome of *field-and-streamer*.

The guide pumped Troy's hand. "Looking to see Mr. Odegard."

He hauled a canvas bag from the river into the boat. Tethered to the dory since morning, it was filled with beer chilled in the water. By the time Gus Odegard appeared, Troy had drunk a couple of Coronas and regaled his new friends with adventures from the life of Edwin Ryan.

"Idaho's a powerful healer," he said, rubbing his sore knee.

"Except for those kids we met, they're having an awful time."

"You hear about that, Mr. Odegard? Kid wiped out at Salmon Falls, lost his raft, sliced his head. He didn't have a chance of getting through this water. We begged them to come down here but they wanted to stay at Bargamin Creek."

"Suspicious types?" Odegard asked.

"Just upset."

"I'll let Corn Creek know they're stranded without a raft," Odegard said.

Troy took a swig of beer. He vaguely remembered a girl and boy on the cliff above Salmon Falls.

"I guess those were the same youngsters we saw," Odegard said. "Black, Mexican, Indian, half-breed of something."

"They look like twins but they're cousins," a guide said. "His family owns a vacation house in Salmon. Nice guy, college kid."

"That was them, all right," Odegard concurred.

"Downstream, we had some luck. We found a black rubber bag and rocket boxes in an eddy. We never saw the raft."

"They were scouting Salmon Falls when we came over in the jetboat. So you left them where?"

"Bargamin, didn't have much choice."

"You should have brought them here."

"They wanted to stay and hike up the creek into the mountains."

Troy leaned against the post of the dock, listening to the guides and Gus Odegard discuss the storm due in. When it was time to push off, the passengers took their seats in the dories. Troy watched them drift toward a wide bend in the river. One by one, the enchanting boats began to glide away.

"Stop!" he called urgently.

"What?" a guide shouted.

"Did she say *where*?"

"Who?" the guide cupped his hands in the wind.

"The girl? Did she say where she came from?"

"New Mexico." The guide mouthed as the dory contacted the swift current.

"New Mexico," Troy said, dragging himself up the small knoll of grass away from the dock. "New Mexico, New Mexico, New Mexico."

39

Bargamin Creek, swollen by the severe winter snow melt, roared over fallen logs, coming hard and fast off the north side of the mountain range that lined most of the Salmon River canyon. A steep path followed the creek north into the Bitterroot Wilderness, eventually leading to Hell's Half Acre in the east and Moose Ridge in the west.

From the entrance to the creek, the beach at Bargamin extended fifty yards, much of it covered by egg-shaped rocks. That was where Quinn and Ruby camped with the party of dories. From eddies, the guides had retrieved a black rubber bag with sleeping gear and food plus three rocket boxes. Without their raft, however, Ruby and Quinn were stranded. They were sure to be susceptible to inquiry, forced to travel overland or hitch a ride downstream or wait for the rangers at Corn Creek to be notified of their marooned condition.

The guides cleaned and bandaged Quinn's cut. They fed them dinner and breakfast. After a night of rest, Quinn's headache and bruises were only dull throbs. He and Ruby conferred. They decided to walk up the Bargamin trail into the mountains and make camp away from river traffic until their food ran out.

As soon as they left the beach behind, their spirits rose. Shaded by ponderosa and fir, lined with wildflowers and huckleberry, the trail followed the creek. When they needed to cool off, like river otters, they plunged into the water. For a couple of hours, with only the sound of birds, the rushing water, and the rhythm of their own footsteps, the primordial world was their own.

"Hey!" a voice whistled.

A few yards off the trail was a young woman, hardly more than a child, seated on a log, fanning a toddler on her lap.

"Sick," she reported, beckoning them closer.

Ruby ran to the creek, dipped her bandanna in the water, and patted the child's face.

"Sick with what?" Quinn asked.

"God's will," she said, raising her eyes to the sky. "Three days with fever."

Quinn scanned the trail, the woods, the mountains in the distance, her waist-long braids, her vest and homemade skirt, her weathered work boots.

"Did you walk here?" he asked.

"I carried him off," she said.

The child swung his arms at his mother's chest.

"There, there," she soothed, hugging his head. "I got to find a doctor."

"Where's a doctor?" Quinn glanced around.

"Truth told, I have no idea," she said.

Quinn unrolled his sleeping bag and spread it by the log. "Put him down," he said.

"I got to hold him. I'm the only thing that keeps him from flying off to God."

Ruby rummaged through their supplies for crackers and dry apples. She boiled water for tea.

"I'm Hazel Jenkins," she said. "This is Lucas Jenkins. We both very thankful."

Lucas's lips sputtered but there was no saliva. He cried but there were no tears. His face was white and splotched, his breath erratic. Hazel wet her finger in a cup of stream water and stuck it in his mouth. At first, he sucked ferociously, then spat up.

"There, there, there," she said.

"We can make camp here," Ruby said. "It's going to rain. You might slip on the trail. You might drop Lucas. Tomorrow, we can help you." She took Hazel's arm. "We'll stay together and take turns watching him tonight."

Quinn strung up a plastic tarp and staked it with willow branches. Under the tarp, he and Ruby put up his father's Army tent. Rain splattered through the trees onto the nylon roof. Wind rattled the trees. The gray sky darkened. The temperature turned brisk. The three sat huddled, quiet and dry, watching Lucas.

40

Ruby slid out of her sleeping bag and untied the tent flap. In the clearing of soft duff and lush ferns, the air was fresh and wet with pine scent, the sky streaked with clouds scudding over the mountain peaks.

"Why would she run away?"

"Too heathen, I guess," Quinn smirked.

"Heathen?" Ruby gulped a laugh. "When was the last time you worshipped false idols?"

"Yesterday!" He raised his hands in surrender.

"Cursed?"

His hands rose higher. "A minute ago!"

"Fornicated?"

A deep blush crossed his face.

"Tell me," she said, twirling her fingers around his hair. "You tell me. I tell you."

"Never," he confessed.

"No, really?"

"Really truly."

"I thought girls jumped you, game boy!"

"Not the right ones."

"You in the closet?"

"Not that either," he shrugged. "Shy, I guess."

Ruby's fantasy of life in California included hordes of sexy young women fighting over Quinn.

"The longer you wait, the shyer you get," she said.

"Pathologically shy," he sighed.

"Everything works?"

"Apparently," he said. "And you?"

"I live in a wasteland. On weekends, dumb low-rider kids get wasted on wine and hippie brats get stoned on pot. Who wants to have sex with a dude who's out of it?"

"I know you've done something," Quinn said. He could read it in her body.

"There's my friend August but he doesn't count. Sometimes I let him hump me. He's like a charity case."

Ruby ached to have love-making sex. Her new life required it.

"It's probably okay to do it once," she said. "Don't they call that 'kissing cousins'?"

Quinn shook as he slipped his arm around Ruby's waist and bent her backwards. They fell on the ground in one graceful motion and Ruby folded underneath him, her heart pounding. She loved the feeling of his weight, the feeling of his creamy skin, the bristles on his chin and cheeks. She and Quinn had always loved each other. He was her childhood groom and she was his bride.

"The last two people on earth," she purred, her lips against his ear.

They lay kissing, lost in the smell and taste of each other. Eager, hungry, wet kisses in a tangle of legs and hips.

"Reckon it's time to stop that!" a voice croaked.

"What the hell!" Quinn leapt to his feet. Ruby rolled over the ground to the nearest tree.

"You seen her?" A small, hairy man with a shotgun stepped out of the woods.

"Last night," Quinn said.

"With the boy?"

"We haven't seen them this morning," Ruby said.

"You lying," the man said.

"No, sir."

"What she tell you?" His deep-set eyes were too tiny to read. "You hear me asking?"

There was a wrong and right answer. Quinn needed Ruby's help.

"Nothing," she said.

"Now you lying!" he shouted.

Ruby and Quinn jumped.

"Lucas was sick," Ruby said. "She wanted to find a doctor."

"Still sick?"

"He looked sick to me," Quinn said.

"You a doctor?"

"No, sir, but he was running a high fever. He couldn't take solids. He couldn't even drink water."

Jenkins regarded the two youngsters. Hard to tell girl from boy. Likely pervert siblings and offspring of sin.

"What she say about me?"

"Excuse me, sir, you are?"

The menacing man with overworked arms and bearded like a troll swung his gun at Ruby. "Her lawful God-fearing husband!"

"No need to point that way, sir," Quinn stammered.

"What she say about me?"

"I don't believe she mentioned you," Quinn said.

"Did she tell you where she came from?"

"Ruby, did Hazel tell us where she came from?"

"She said there was a camp but no doctor."

Quinn cringed.

"She done trade the devil for a witch." Jenkins waved the gun. "She done told you. Now you know."

"We don't know anything, I swear," Quinn said.

"Don't tolerate swearing," Jenkins said.

41

New Mexico.

All over again, Troy hated Ruby Ryan. Everything about her reminded him of Charlene. Both of them curses that wouldn't go away.

"What's got him?" Odegard asked.

Dom didn't know. His orders were to prepare supplies for an excursion to Bargamin Creek.

"One day, he can't get off the chair. Next day, he's ready to go."

Gus Odegard didn't like Edwin Ryan. Although he looked Gus in the eye, it wasn't a real look. Nor did he really listen. On the other hand, Gus liked Dom a lot. There was nothing to suggest they were related. Adopted, he figured.

"You disturbing the wildlife!" Odegard yelled. "Hunting season ain't started. You read the rules, ain't you?"

Troy didn't stop shooting at the water until Dom had loaded their pack on the Lazy OK's jetboat. The jog upstream was brief. The boat bounced over the rapids and pulled alongside the rock-littered beach at Bargamin Creek. Early afternoon, the beach was empty. Rafting parties camped the night before had departed. New parties wouldn't arrive for a few hours.

Dom lay the pack down and started to make camp.

"Boy, this ain't the place to rest. Best to go up the creek."

Dom hoisted the pack on his back and headed up the trail. The day was overcast and, according to Odegard, predicted to get colder and wetter by evening.

"How far you want to go?" Dom asked, toiling like a burro.

The hairs on Troy's neck stiffened. He was in no mood to talk. He was agitated and preoccupied. The serene forest glade and forecast of more rain did not improve his mood. Nor the chatter of Dom Gambolli.

"I hate to cross your opinion, Uncle Edwin."

"Shut up!"

"But the beach is better for camping. Easier to shelter when it rains. It's not good sense to start trudging up this way. For what?"

"A half-nigger bastard girl," Troy muttered.

"I don't like that language. It's intolerant."

"You got that right!" Troy swiped at the mosquito on his cheek. "Something came back to me. The girl we saw at Salmon Falls?"

Dom nodded. He'd seen her. Pretty and statuesque, she looked like a goddess poised over the falls as if she could fly.

"She's the one!" Troy said.

"Here?" Dom's unibrow lifted doubtfully.

"Always go with your hunch."

"I guess it's possible," Dom said.

From limited experience, he had learned that many unexpected and farfetched things were possible. His cousin, the smartest member of the Gambolli family, had studied astrophysics at MIT. He told Dom that *everything* was possible if you lived long enough.

They marched steadily up the incline, Troy cursing Ruby under his breath with every painful step. He had to find and squash her. About that, he had no doubt.

"Knee itches like a son-of-a-bitch," he yelled at Dom.

Troy slapped the scab to make it quit but it was useless. He stripped and slid down the bank into one of Bargamin's cold refreshing pools.

Downstream Dom fished. Fishing calmed and cleared his mind. Clearest of all were his impressions of Edwin Ryan. Unpredictable, bent, and maybe bona fide crazy. As soon as the caper on Bargamin Creek was finished, Dom planned to catch the next jetboat to Riggins.

"Hey!" Troy called to a woman with a bundle in her arms, struggling down the path and praying loudly.

"Good Lord!" Hazel shrilled. She staggered backwards and shielded her eyes from the sight of a naked man. After three years of marriage, she'd never seen her husband naked.

"Don't go!" Troy shouted.

"Please, no!" she shrieked.

Thigh-deep in water, Dom's concentration shut out everything except the colorful bobbing fly. He was supremely content.

"Grab that woman!" Troy yelled.

"Please, no!" Hazel stumbled on the path.

"Dom!" Troy barked.

Dom was startled from his reverie. Contentment vanished. He placed the rod and fly box on a flat rock and hopped up the bank to block the path.

"God's will," Hazel screamed. "Are you a doctor?"

"No, ma'am."

"What are you then?" she asked.

"Nothing yet," Dom admitted.

"Is the other man a doctor?"

"No, ma'am."

"What is he?"

"He knows a lot about cars," Dom said.

"My child needs a doctor."

Troy appeared fully clothed. "Excuse me, ma'am, I didn't mean for anyone to notice me."

"I got to find a doctor," she panted.

"There's a ways to go before you reach the river," Dom said.

"How far?" She didn't have much reserve left.

"At the river, somebody will take you downstream to Mr. Odegard's place. He'll call the rangers and whatever else you need," Dom said.

"You reckon?"

Dom stepped forward. "I can carry the child."

Hazel smiled although unaccustomed to strangers and kindness.

"We're on a mission from God," Troy explained, intercepting Lucas and returning the boy to his mother's arms.

"I am too," Hazel asserted.

"We got twelve to twenty-four hours to find a girl," Troy said. "It's a matter of life and death."

"Mine is matters of life and death too," Hazel said.

"We understand she might be on this trail. She's a colored girl." Troy dropped his voice. "I'm from the World Disease Convention Center in Orlando. You heard of that?"

"I heard of Orlando," Hazel said.

"I'm sorry I'm not a doctor." Troy dabbed at the perspiration on his upper lip. "I'm a tracker."

"A tracker?" Dom asked, torn between belief and disbelief.

"We got high classified clearance security to believe this girl could have a deadly disease."

"She was there last night," Hazel cried out and pointed to the trail. "We slept next to each other. My boy, sick and all, will he catch it?"

Troy put his hand on Hazel's shoulder. His thoughts ran faster than a greased pig, which in Troy Mason's case was not a figure of speech. He actually knew how fast a greased pig ran. He'd tackled one at his seventh-grade picnic and won a clock radio.

"You have to be intimate," he said.

42

At first, Kate was terrified by the sound, the chop, the rapids. Adrift in a rubber boat at the mercy of the currents, she was filled with foreboding that she would not survive the River of No Return. But after a day, she surrendered her fate to the river and David's skill. After two days, she was exuberant. A buoyancy sprang up inside her as she realized she had no control. Even better, she had no illusion of control. She'd let go and accepted whatever there was as long as it kept her moving toward Ruby.

At Salmon Falls, the great rush of water excited the appropriate degree of terror. Per David's instructions, she clung to the bowlines and shut her eyes. His skill was superb, the river merciful. They proceeded rapidly, scanning beaches, groves of trees, elevated mountain pastures. At each campsite, they stopped to inquire if anyone had seen a young brown couple.

No one had seen them.

They stopped at Bargamin Creek to camp. A large rafting party was spread along the beach, tents pitched, dinner in preparation. Passengers relaxed with cold beer and chilled wine. Laughter, singing, mandolin, and guitar floated over the water. An osprey soared above them, a trout in its talons. On the high ridges, bighorn sheep grazed beneath the gray rumbling sky.

Kate and David picked their way around the rookery of egg-shaped rocks to a secluded area of beach near the confluence of river and creek. They ate a simple dinner of nuts, raisins, and cheese, and collapsed on the sand.

Kate stared at the stars. "The firmament," she said.

David smiled with exhaustion. "*Between firmament and firmament, Jehovah created earth.*"

"Bible studies, doctor?"

"Torah," he said. David had given up the God of his fathers. At thirteen after his Bar Mitzvah, he declared himself an atheist.

Their eyes roamed the night sky's wonders. He took Kate's hand. It was her wonderment that refreshed him. If not God and heaven, he guessed she believed in something.

The following afternoon, David pulled ashore at the Lazy OK, a working ranch of fifty acres on the south side of the river with cattle, sheep, trail horses for guests, chickens, pigs, goats, and dogs. Ten years ago, the third-generation descendant of the original settler froze to death in a late spring snowstorm. When the Lazy OK was put up for sale, Gus Odegard sold his sporting goods store in Coeur d'Alene and bought it.

David and Kate climbed the rock stairs to the lodge. A beautiful spot in a succession of beautiful spots. Odegard pointed behind the screen door to a cooler of ice cream and beer, shelves of candy, chips, and gum. There was also the dining area for a late lunch or early dinner. On a chalkboard was printed *Grilled Mountain Trout, French Fries, Coleslaw, Chocolate Pudding.*

Ice cream in hand, they took seats beside Odegard in rocking chairs that overlooked the river and far mountain ridge.

"I was here twenty years ago," David said. "Glad to see it hasn't changed."

"We used to bring our kids out every summer. When my wife died and the old timer passed away, I figured out a way to buy it. You might say I bought a dream. Not many men claim that." Odegard sipped his coffee. "Where you two from?"

"Land of Enchantment," Kate smiled. "New Mexico's got stiff competition here in Idaho."

Odegard was surprised. He figured them for big city people.

"I got a couple of guests from New Mexico staying here right now. I expect they'd agree with you, especially the kid."

"Kid?" Kate trembled.

"Folks coming from as far away as France and Japan, they never seen beautiful like this." Odegard's eyes misted.

"Kid, you said?" Kate repeated.

"A college kid."

"Quinn Bass, would that be his name?"

"No, Dominic."

The trio gazed over the river. In the canyon, light dwindled slowly. Even with the mounting layer of clouds, dusk would last a long time.

"Didn't happen to see a raft hung up?" Odegard asked. "Dories come through and reported a couple of kids lost theirs going over Salmon Falls." He snapped his fingers. "There's always trouble when a youngster gets on the river and thinks him and God going to figure everything out."

Kate gripped the arms of the rocking chair. "Where are they?"

"Bargamin Creek, you would have passed it," Odegard said. "Prettiest spot on the river after this one. Of course, everyone's entitled to an opinion. They should have brought them down here. But they refused to come. They'll show up when the food runs out. That, I guarantee."

"We were just at Bargamin," Kate said.

"You two welcome to stay here. We got two empty places since my New Mexico fellows went up to Bargamin today."

"We'd like to try to get back to Bargamin ourselves," David said. "If we can hire out your jetboat to run us up there, we'll go right now."

"Seems like Bargamin is the charm of the day." Odegard rubbed his chin. "Once Mr. Ryan heard about the accident, all he could jaw on was Bargamin."

"Ryan?" Kate dug her fingernails into David's thigh.

"Edwin Ryan and his nephew, Dom, the ones from New Mexico. Mr. Ryan ain't my kind of people, but it takes all kinds. The kid's an extra nice fellow except he don't eat meat. Some crazy thing out in the world every day. That's why I like it right here."

"Ryan?" David caught Odegard's eye. "Edwin Ryan, you're sure?"

"Sure, I'm sure. That's what I'm telling you. Ever since the dories was here, big Ryan got possessed. He hadn't moved from the porch the whole time on account of a busted knee. But this morning, nothing could stop him. He had to go hiking if it was the last thing he did."

43

After David and Kate untied their raft and unloaded their gear from the jetboat, Odegard roared away. They moored the raft and made a pile of their supplies. Parties of rafters had again claimed most of the beach. David and Kate asked guides and passengers if they'd seen a young brown couple or a man hobbling around. They'd seen no one going up the path along the creek or coming down.

Once again, David and Kate pitched camp on the east side of the beach at the creek's mouth. It was a cheerless evening, the air clammy with the foretaste of rain. They ate dinner out of cans and crawled into the tent before daylight had completely disappeared.

"Ruby's probably dead," Kate said forlornly. "Troy found and killed her."

"He can barely walk, Kate. He has no idea where they went. The kid he bamboozled, Mr. Odegard says he's okay. Ruby can outrun and outwit him. Quinn is young and strong. You have to believe," David added, surprised by his own conviction.

Kate lay in her sleeping bag, trying to quiet her nightmare thoughts. When she finally drifted into sleep, it was fitful. No more than an hour passed before she awoke. She'd heard movements near the deep channel of the creek. She listened, trying to hear above the noise of the river. There was a rustling in the brush and a high, almost human groan.

"Bear," she shook David's arm.

"Bear?" David was sleepy, muddled with dreams.

He pulled on a pair of sweats and grabbed his glasses and flashlight. He advanced from the tent toward the creek with a heavy branch. Kate heard him shuffle away. There were his steps and another animal, a cry, a moan, even words.

"David!" she whispered, staring out at the darkness, listening for shouts and scuffles, resistance or retreat.

He emerged, stepping over the uneven ground with something in his arms. Following him was a young woman in a long skirt and quilted vest.

Carefully, he laid the bundle on top of his sleeping bag. "Lucas, Lucas," he said, palpating the child's stomach while Lucas cried in feeble protest. His lips were cracked, his belly hard, his tongue enlarged. The lymph nodes in his neck, armpits, and groin swollen and his pale sere skin blotched with even paler dots.

Hazel stared wide-eyed at David and Kate. She was afraid. She had left the Realm of Truth and reached the perimeter of what her husband called the Kingdom of Doubt.

"What's wrong with him?" Kate asked.

"God's will," Hazel said weakly.

"How much water has he taken?" David asked.

"He can't keep none down," Hazel said.

"Hydrate," David pronounced.

"You licensed?" Hazel asked in a girl's voice, trying to sound grown-up.

"I am," he said humbly.

"Then you have to save him! Save him, doctor, save him!"

Her pleas only raised David's doubts. He had not always been able to save.

"Can you save him?" she yanked his elbow.

"I've got to think what's best."

Kate reached for her medicine bag. "Comfrey tea?"

"Make the tea," David agreed.

He wrapped Lucas in a wool sweater and wiped his head with a wet rag. After the comfrey tea had cooled, Hazel dipped her finger in a thermos cup and slipped it into Lucas's mouth. He sucked, then gagged.

"Try it, baby," she begged.

"Come with me," David said to Kate.

They moved across the beach. Gumdrops of sap stuck to the bottoms of their shoes, their Tevas lifting in slow-motion as if glued to the sand. At the raft, David loosened the hoopie from a black rubber bag. Kate held the flashlight as he rummaged until he found his first aid kit. Inside were packets of syringes, lengths of rubber tubing, needles both 25-gauge and butterfly, and plastic prescription cylinders marked in pink block letters, HER and FEN.

Kate's eyes fell on a baggy labeled HM. "That was your shit that almost killed Ruby?"

"Not killed," he said.

"Those days when I believed dealers had raided my house, looking for shit and taking my daughter, it was *your* shit?"

"I know, Kate."

"You let me believe that."

"We didn't know anything, Kate. She could have been taken."

Her hand rose to slap him.

"A few things went missing," David said. "I guessed it was teenagers."

"But you *saw* the baggy and admitted no part."

"Kate," he pleaded. They were lame, his excuses.

"Shut up," she said.

At the tent, they boiled water for a saline-glucose solution. When it was cool, David filled a water bottle. He placed a section of duct tape over the opening of the bottle and jammed a two-foot tube through a nick in the tape, sucking the end to start the drip flowing. After tying off Lucas's arm, he thumped the crook of his elbow for veins. With the butterfly needle's small bore, he calculated he could make the hit but as he eased the needle into a vein, Lucas jerked. Hazel pinned down the arm and held it steady. David eased the needle in again. He waited for the flashback of blood and pressed the needle in place until he was certain blood was flowing. Then, securing the needle, he taped it down and fastened the tubing to the butterfly's tail.

His hands worked deftly but he was shaky. He feared whatever he tried would fail. Once, in California, he failed and the child died.

44

Two hours later, they reached the fire road that intersected the creek trail. At the juncture was a view of a small valley and beyond the trees and stream, a steep forested hillside and taller mountains mottled with lodgepole pines. They turned on the fire road that rolled along the ridge.

Beside a quartzite boulder, Justice Jenkins stopped. The boulder was cracked into two symmetrical V-shaped halves with a wedge large enough for a large man. This was the entrance to the camp. On the other side of the rock, a path led to a hollow where trees had been cut to make a clearing. Beyond the stumps in the shade of Western red cedars, firs, and an Engelmann spruce were a dozen tents, two majestic tepees, an M4A2 Sherman tank, picnic tables, portable outhouse, folding chairs, and electric generator.

Two youth lay on blankets listening to a portable CD player. The only distinguishable sound was "Heil Hitler!" Whenever they heard it, they mumbled lazily, "Heil Hitler!"

"Are you prepared to defend yourselves?" Justice Jenkins bellowed.

They jerked, jumped, stood, saluted. "Yes, sir!"

Jenkins returned the salute, signaled for a chair, and pointed a finger at a girl with a pinched joyless face.

"Breakfast," he barked. "Rations for the spies."

"We aren't spies!" Ruby defended.

"We know what you are." Jenkins's eyes narrowed to pinpoints.

The girl assembled cups of water and a plastic plate of graham crackers for rations. "Who are they really?" she asked.

"They helped Hazel. They helped her get the boy away."

Another girl emerged from a tent, balancing a tray and walking slowly so the water in the bowl didn't spill. Beside the bowl was an heirloom shaving brush made of silvertip badger bristles, a cup of granulated lavender soap, a washcloth, and a large bottle of Listerine. She held a mirror as Jenkins scrubbed his skin with the cloth, lathered the soap, shaved the stubble around his beard and muttonchops, gargled, and spat the mouthwash on the ground.

"They came up in the woods spooking and spying. Ain't that right?"

"No, sir," Ruby interjected.

"But I believe we can use them," Jenkins said.

His comment elicited a murmur of approval from the cadets. *Use* spoke to fantasies of both pleasure and pain.

"I heard *this* was once a free country. Maybe you heard the same? *One nation under God.* These days, it's only free if you born nigger, Mexican, queer, or Jew. You listening?"

Quinn and Ruby listened intently.

"Tell you a story," he blinked. Where there should have been eyes were two fringed dashes. "First time, I set foot in Idaho, the roads were closed because of snow. More snow than the continent of Antarctica. Which tells you something, don't it? What's it tell you?" His eyes riveted on the cadets.

They shook their heads.

"Ignorant scum," he said.

"I'm not a drinking man now but I was drinking then. I headed to a bar to sit out the storm." Jenkins's eyelids lifted slightly. "You listening?"

Everyone looked alert.

"They got pizza in this bar. Thick pizza, thin pizza, pizza with wop names like Neapolitan and Sicilian. I eyed them, trying to decide which to eat. I like to know what I'm putting inside me. That's a good thing." Justice Jenkins patted his belly. "I asked the bartender if the thick crust had more yeast. He thought a minute and then said something that changed me forever. They call that 'epiphany.' You boys heard of epiphany?"

The cadets had not.

"He said, 'Yeast is life and salt is the antithesis of life.' You boys know what 'antithesis' means?"

They did not. They were clueless when it came to Justice Jenkins's questions. Hawk-faced and crank-skinny with muscles like knotted socks, dressed in camouflage fatigues, Red Wing boots, soiled wife-beater T-shirts, they'd run away from home, enticed by a pamphlet which claimed it would train them to defend white people against invaders.

They'd been in Jenkins's camp for a week. So far, they'd washed dishes and listened to him blabber. They'd been forced to read the Bible. Much to their dismay, alcohol and drugs were prohibited. Although they had fair expertise at getting around rules, their smoke and drink had been confiscated at the V-shaped boulder. There was nothing to puff on but wild weeds. Promised training in weapon handling and martial arts, they'd not been permitted to shoot once.

"I was once a bona fide corpse. You listening?"

The cadets had already heard this story. They'd been told it was one of Justice Jenkins's *teaching* stories. They didn't know what that meant either.

"Declared dead by the U.S. of America, White House, Pentagon, and the rich Jews in Hollywood."

The cadets hooted their disdain.

Quinn scrutinized the pimpled rubes. One had shaved his head and on the crown was a swastika tattooed in the center of a ring of fire. The other resembled an Easter chick, covered in bright blond hair that sprouted along the rim of his ears, the back of his neck, over his head and face, and on his fingers. His arms were matted with yellow tufts. He had a swastika on his arm and H-A-T-E and L-O-V-E on his knuckles.

"My bride got the news I was a goner. Army reported to my folks they had a hero for a son. Jet plane sent them a body to bury and a big flag as a souvenir. They put a nice gravestone in the dirt where I went under. My wife remarried. My folks hung my photo over the TV. They thought that was the end of me, but I came home." Jenkins parted his two scrolls of moustache. "I resurrected like the Son of God. I reckon I maybe got three more lives to go. What you boys think we should do with these mutts?"

45

In late spring, Justice Jenkins and his two brothers, Henry and Eli, stole a thirty-two-ton flatbed truck from an I-40 rest stop west of Albuquerque. It wasn't difficult. At one time or another, they'd all run stolen vehicles. They'd all done time. When the XXX-sized driver came into the empty john, Henry, the youngest, brawniest, and most vicious, clobbered him with a Louisville Slugger. Then they gagged and bound him in a closed stall, taped a sign, broken, on the door, nailed it shut, ran the truck up to Manny's chop-shop in Espanola, refashioned its identity overnight, and drove east on 64 to I-25, home free. The truck was exactly what they needed to haul a tank into a remote area of Idaho, north of the Main Fork of the Salmon River.

Manny accompanied them to Carmen where he took over the truck and drove it back to Espanola. During the course of three nights, the brothers guided the tank at a snail's pace over fire roads to a piece of liberated U.S. Forest Service land which they renamed "Patriot Park." This was to be a summer training outpost with tents for lodging and the tank for defense. Young women they had, either wives or cousins. Young men, they planned to recruit from Aryan enclaves in the Northwest. Joab and Absalom were brought in from Spokane. Joab and Absalom weren't their birth names but commando names given when Justice Jenkins baptized them in Bargamin Creek.

"Where are the pagan boys?" Justice asked Joab.

"They asked to be excused, sir."

"This ain't elementary school," Justice sneered. "This is life. You want to be *excused* from life?"

"No, sir," Joab said.

"Like you have to make pee pee?"

A tow-haired child giggled as Jenkins gave him a wink.

"Even Goshen knows what that means. Nothing excuses you from the Lord's work, day in and day out."

"They asked Captain Eli, sir," Absalom stammered.

"Who's in charge here?" Jenkins stroked the sheath that held his Winchester riot knife. Even naked, he kept it around his waist, its blade ideal for scalping. So far, that hadn't come up.

"Commander Justice!"

They could not be blamed for his brother, Eli. Eli had independent tendencies. He liked to wander in the woods and commune with natural splendors. He liked to quote Henry David Thoreau. He had inclinations that weren't altogether Christian.

Attention turned when Eli Jenkins stepped from the woods, his stature and demeanor suggesting a man who couldn't possibly be related to Justice. Justice was a potbellied gnome. Eli was tall and rail-thin with loose white hair and clean-shaven except for a caprine tuft. He leaned forward as he limped into the clearing. He was barefoot and had a deep scratch across the instep.

Behind him strode three robust young men, each dragging a sledge loaded with wood. Slung on their backs were cloth sacks filled with wild berries and wild onions. They wore cargo pants, Minnetonka fringed moccasins, Raiders caps, and their bare torsos, necks, and arms were covered with intricate tattoos.

"Ran into a couple of mutts," Justice said.

Eli glanced at Ruby and Quinn. "Now we got to feed them," he said, wiping his hands on his coveralls.

"We ain't got to do nothing," Justice chuckled.

"The girl, she looks strong," he said admiringly.

"Reminds you of Lucille, don't she?"

Lucille was Eli's second wife, half-Irish, half-Cherokee. She died in a 1990 Chevy Blazer after it crashed into a semi and rebounded against the pier of an interstate bridge. The steering wheel crushed her. Eli retrieved their drugs, hopped over the guardrail, crossed the bridge, hid in a field, and a few hours later, hitchhiked from the scene of the accident, north to Sacramento. Southbound was tied up for hours due to the accident. The next day, Eli read that the driver had bled to death. It was one thing he never forgave himself for, although he believed God forgave him.

"They helped Hazel," Justice said.

"You found Hazel?"

"She spent the night with them and took off in the morning to the river." Justice chewed the inside of his cheek. His cheek was raw from twelve hours of chewing. Now he'd have to go down the hill to find her.

Eli's three acolytes unloaded and stacked the wood. Quinn stared at their backs as they worked. He was familiar with tattoos of the Maori and Yakuza clans. But the elaborate patterns on the young men of wheels, runes, labyrinths, and the letters EK were mysteries.

Justice watched their arms lift and sort. His joints ached looking at them. He suffered from arthritis in his right hip. He'd been told he needed a hip replacement but surgery frightened him. Several family members had died under the knife. He believed they'd been murdered.

"I wasn't here so they used you," Justice said to Eli. "I hear they asked to be *excused* from Bible studies."

Eli dipped from a can of Skoal Straight, tucking the snuff between his gum and lip. As soon as the saliva mixed with the tobacco, a light sugar high rushed through his bloodstream.

"They're frisky, Justice. You got to let them work it off. If they don't work it off in the woods, they going to work it off somewhere else. Anyway they got way more sense than the numbskulls from Spokane. They're useful and they don't complain."

"They ain't Christian, Eli," Justice said. "Once they get to be Christian, I won't mind."

"Snorri says they hate and love the same things as Christians."

"I ain't sure about that."

"Snorri, he's the intelligent one. He can quote Shakespeare."

"Snorri don't sound intelligent. It sounds like Seven Dwarfs."

"It's from Iceland."

"That's an unnatural heathen place," Justice said. "They got darkness all day in winter and sun all night in summer."

"He can tell stories about the original Snorri. You seen the Mjolnir on his palm? It goes in four directions like the cross but it didn't originate in suffering. It belonged to Thor. It's Thor's hammer of strength, thundering in heaven."

"You aim on conversion?" Justice laughed.

"I aim on the Lord's knowledge," Eli said.

Eli Jenkins had heard of Odin and Asatru on the street. He knew it was popular in prisons. As for the "14 Words" tattooed on each of the boys—*We must secure the existence of our people and a future for White Children*—there was no conflict with Christian belief.

"That's their motto. Hitler's motto too," Eli said.

"Hitler's only half the equation," Justice argued. "You got to have salvation. That's how Christians balance civilization. Pagans ain't civilized or balanced. They make blood sacrifices to false gods. They speak in false tongues. Either those boys put Jesus in their hearts or they go back to Seattle."

The three EK youth stood across the clearing. They were tired and content. They'd had a good day in the woods. They liked living out of the city close to Thule and the great sacred trees and sacred river. They also liked Eli Jenkins. He listened to them. He asked questions about the ancient marks that blanketed their bodies. He showed respect.

They did not like his brother, Justice, who raved on about Jesus. Among themselves, they'd discussed an Icelandic coup. They would take Commander Justice down and raise Captain Eli up. The plan was Snorri's. Snorri was in charge. He was a *skald*. He quoted from the *Elder Edda* and *Younger Edda*. He had certified proof that noble *skald* blood ran in his veins. The other two couldn't read but they liked hearing Snorri tell the stories of war and gods. He taught them how to play *Swords and Shields*. They looked up to Snorri. He could shoot a bow as good as a gun. It was Captain Eli who let Snorri bring his bow into camp.

46

"You supposed to treat us like Geneva," Ruby said.

"Geneva?" Justice could only recall a gas station he'd once robbed in Geneva, Indiana.

"There are rules to play fair."

Jenkins's laugh was friendly. "You talking Golden Rule?"

Do unto others, Kate always said that. She tried to be fair. Too fair, Ruby thought. *As you would have them . . .*

"Golden Rule to spy," Justice said.

"We don't do that," Ruby protested.

"You spying now," he grimaced.

Eli sauntered into the clearing. He had changed into sun-dried jeans, a denim shirt, and red bandanna. On his head was a Stetson with a rattlesnake band. He was still barefoot, his cut bandaged, his amber toenails gnarled, his heels toughened like hooves.

"What you doing with them?" he asked.

"Wringing out the truth," Justice said, placing a well-thumbed Bible in Quinn's hand. "Full name."

"Quinn Ryan Bass," he mumbled.

"Race?"

"Race is a false construct," Quinn said. He'd studied the invention of whiteness in the aftermath of Bacon's Rebellion in 1676.

"Race?" Eli repeated.

"Other," Quinn said.

"That'll do. Write them both down as *Other*."

"Family religion?" Eli asked, lifting his mirrored aviator sunglasses.

"Baptist," Quinn said.

"Is that normal Baptist or nigger Baptist?" Justice winked at the cadets. "Fainting, fanning, hollering, snakes, speaking in tongues?"

Quinn wished he had the courage to leap on Justice's neck and rip out his tongue. It was the most violent urge that had ever possessed him. No doubt a suicide mission for him and a death warrant for Ruby.

"Baptist that is *no respecter of persons*," Quinn said.

No respecter of persons, Justice had never heard the phrase. He liked it.

"Student of what?" Eli asked.

Quinn stretched the truth. "Engineering," he said.

The brothers nodded their approval. It was an asset to have an engineer on any operation.

Eli passed the Bible to Ruby. She opened it randomly and read.

> *Rescue me, O my God, from the hand of the wicked, from the grasp of the unjust and cruel man.*

Jenkins grabbed it and flipped to Ezekiel 16.

> *Have you not committed lewdness in addition to all your abominations? Behold, every one who uses proverbs will use this proverb about you, 'Like mother, like daughter.'*

"You don't know my mother!" Ruby cried.

"I see the fruit of her labor."

"You see nothing," Ruby spat.

"Wildcat," Eli throbbed with admiration.

"Name and occupation?"

She deferred to Quinn. "Ruby Rosen Ryan, high-school dropout."

"Mother's religion?"

"Buddhish," she smiled.

"Buddhish," Eli chortled.

Justice Jenkins combed his beard with his forefinger. He was indecisive. Eli's doubt made him more indecisive.

"Send them back to the river," Eli said.

"To the brig!" Justice shouted obstinately.

Joab poked Ruby and Quinn with a billy club, directing them to the hatch of the tank and down the gangway into a rusty hull. It was stifling hot and stank of oil. Armed with club, whistle, and megaphone, Joab stood guard at the top of the hatch, practicing to be a warrior.

After fifteen minutes, he was drowsy and bored. He slouched against the turret. He shut his eyes and let his legs and boots dangle into the open hatch.

At suppertime, the prisoners were ordered out of the tank and seated between Justice and Eli. Eli delivered his blessing on the food and a prosperous future for Patriot Park. At the end of the blessing, he sang a hymn and fondled Ruby's head. The camp cadets and the three pagans sat around the table with a half-dozen children. The camp's women did not sit. They stood nearby with platters of lumpy rice, canned corn and peas, and a huckleberry crumble for dessert.

Halfway through the crumble, they heard a shot from the direction of the fire road. The women grabbed the children and fled to the woods where they'd been instructed to hide in case of invasion. Justice and Eli sprinted up the path. Eli carried a double-barrel shotgun. Justice had his riot knife in one hand and Army handgun in the other. Justice could run like an Olympian in an emergency. It was the only time he was pain-free.

Minutes later, the brothers and Shem, the camp's chief cadet, appeared with two men, hands tied behind their backs and shackled together with ankle cuffs.

Ruby swooned onto Quinn's shoulder.

"I thought I accidentally killed you!"

"Accidental, my ass," Troy's eyes boiled.

A frightened Dom appraised the quasi-military dress of the cadets, the Asatru skinheads, the Sherman tank, and the alarmed teenage women with infants and toddlers who'd crept back to the perimeter of the camp. Finally his eyes singled out Ruby and Quinn.

"The girl with the disease?" he asked.

"Shut up!" Troy hissed.

"I found them at Bargamin," Shem said. "When I asked if they seen a woman and small child, him," indicating Troy, "responded, 'Yo no.' The other dude, 'Yo yeah.' Then, numero one kicked numero two in the balls."

Justice had Shem untie Dom's hands and hand him the Bible. Dom pinched his nose to test if he was dreaming. He'd often used the pinch test but only once had he actually been asleep.

"Dominic Angelo Gambolli," Dom said.

"Religion?" Eli prompted.

"Catholic, sir."

Disapprobation ran through Patriot Park. Catholic was as bad as Jew. Even the small children recognized these as dirty words.

"Is Dominic a *lazy* boy's name?"

Justice Jenkins was toying with him, the cadets knew that. They'd been toyed with too. It was part of the training.

"It's Italian, sir. Everyone calls me 'Dom.'"

"Do you also answer to dago, guinea, wop, and goombah?" Justice asked.

"That's not a fair question, sir," Dom said.

The others waited for a reaction. A slap, a punch, a whipping with a belt? However, Justice Jenkins approved of Dominic Gambolli's honesty. They also knew his approval was double-edged.

"Are you related to anyone present?"

"I been saying he's my uncle." Dom looked at Troy.

Troy focused solely on Ruby. Like predator on prey, he'd now have his chance.

"Is your relationship a fact?" Justice Jenkins asked, demonstrating to his followers what it took to get at the truth. Most of all, patience. Patience was more reliable than torture. Justice had been tortured and he'd lied.

"No, sir," Dom said.

"Is it a lie?"

"I guess so," Dom admitted.

Jenkins frowned. He blamed himself for these intrusions. He had been distracted by domestic strife and Lucas's illness. He blamed Hazel. She'd run off to the outside world and left a trail behind for everyone to follow.

Troy eagerly laid his hand on the Bible. "Edwin Ryan, Texan, employed as private tracker, Christian born and raised, called to Church of Christ." He knew exactly who he was. "E-d-w-i-n and R-y-a-n," he spelled it out.

"Edwin Ryan is my cousin's honorable name which he stole, sir," Quinn objected. "Ruby, show them your dad's ID bracelet."

Ruby held out her wrist.

"No, she stole that bracelet from me," Troy said.

The commander turned to Dominic, a boy with genuine American appeal, healthy skin, glossy dark hair, and an expression in his eye that was direct.

"Mr. Gambolli, what you think?"

"Me, sir?"

"Let's start at the beginning. Where do you live?"

"Albuquerque, sir."

"Your parents?"

"My parents are Big Angelo and Patty. They own a pizza restaurant near the university, sir."

"They make thick crust and thin crust?"

"Thin, thick, Neapolitan, Sicilian, New York style, and Chicago deep dish. Chicago is the house specialty."

"Do you know about pizza's sacred formula?" Justice asked him.

Dom admitted he did not. "I'm vegan, sir. I don't eat meat or cheese or anything that ever had a mother."

"Plain tomato sauce without cheese, that don't cut it," Justice said.

"Probably not, sir."

"Believe it or not, pizza has been a very special gift in my life," he said.

"I believe it, sir."

Justice Jenkins often invoked pizza in his teachings. Pizza was a universal. It worked as a metaphor for both part and whole. The entire pie, that was the organism. The pieces, plain or embellished with toppings, were individuals. How the pieces fit into the whole, that was the social organization. How the whole created an indivisible entity, that was religion. Pizza's appeal crossed generations. Its flavors satisfied most palettes. It could be used as a topo map, a battleground, and a spiritual force field. The boxes also came in handy for target practice.

"I like Italians," Justice said. "They have Jesus in their heart. They have a whole lot of other crap too but let's say I-ti is okay by me. They make good jokes and racing cars. Most of all, they invented pizza. How the heck did you get mixed up with these folks?"

Dom pointed at Quinn and Ruby. "I don't know them, sir."

"And Mr. Ryan?"

"Last year, my car broke down in Bakersfield. He got me going again. Then, out of the blue, he called me a few days ago. He wondered if I could drive him to Idaho. I thought it might be fun."

"Wasn't it?" Troy commented.

"Down at Lazy OK, that's fun."

"You meet a woman and small child?"

"Late afternoon, we saw them."

"Looking for a goddamn doctor?" Jenkins blasphemed under his breath.

"Mr. Ryan said we couldn't help them. We didn't have time because of the girl." Dom regarded Ruby with pity. "She's got a global disease."

Justice Jenkins's small eyes fixed on Ruby. He directed Eli to include in the notes, "Ruby Rosen Ryan contaminated."

Ruby started to cry out but Snorri caught her attention. A movement of his hand sufficed to warn her. It was as if he were saying that he'd handle it. During supper, he never took his eyes off her. She refused to look at him but she felt him burn a hole in her with his mind.

"Where's your real daddy now?" Justice asked Ruby.

She twisted the bracelet around her wrist. "Dead," she said.

47

By dawn, Lucas's fever was gone. His face had color. He smiled and laughed. Breakfast was oatmeal with brown sugar and hot tea. They ate, listening to the soft thud of rain, Hazel humming and rocking Lucas as he licked her fingers.

She touched the star around David's neck. Brushed gold on a gold link chain, a Bar Mitzvah gift from his grandmother that he only wore on the river.

"It's a Jewish star," David said.

"Jews killed Jesus," Hazel said.

David rose and stepped into the drizzle. He rubbed his eyes and cursed.

"Is he okay?" she asked Kate.

"Jesus *was* Jewish," Kate said. "The Last Supper is a Jewish holiday."

Hazel's eyes closed. She was easily confused in the Kingdom of Doubt.

"It hurts Jewish people to hear that kind of talk. Millions of Jews were murdered by Nazis. Members of David's family were murdered, you understand?"

Hazel had heard Justice speak about Nazis. She understood they were part of the Savior's plan.

"My husband talks about that," she said, stroking Lucas's head.

Leaving camp challenged Justice Jenkins's truths. Putting faith in man above the Lord's design was a sin. Lucas's fever had caused her to defy her husband. Truth told, defiance and doubt scared her more than Mr. Jenkins.

"Jesus hears lies same as truth and judges accordingly," Hazel said. "What I told the girl up the creek, no matter what she done, Jesus already knows it. Jesus forgives."

"Was that Ruby?"

"Ruby, yes, Ruby and Quinn."

"Ruby is my girl," Kate said.

"You here to claim them?" Hazel asked.
"That's right."
Hazel's eyes closed again. "My husband probably got them now."

48

Inside the tank, the hands and ankles of the captives were tied. Quinn stretched out while Ruby sat beside him, sunk against the wall. The air was humid like a sauna and moisture pearled on every surface. Ruby tried to rest but penetrating the semi-darkness were Troy's ice-blue eyes.

"Something bothering you, Ruby," Troy said.

"You *really* know her?" Dom asked.

"I know her name is Ruby Rosen Ryan. I know she lives in Zamora, New Mexico."

"What did my mom ever see in you!"

Troy's teeth gleamed. "Your mom likes men, Ruby. She likes doing special things with them. Special dirty things you starting to learn with August in the back of the truck."

"Shut up," Quinn groaned.

"I believe," Dom said.

"I know what you believe, dingo," Troy said. "I got cramps listening to it day and night. What I tell you?"

Dom couldn't recall.

"Killing gives man an occupation and distraction. Men eat animals so they don't have to kill other men."

"But I believe," Dom started again.

Troy butted the young man with his head and split his lip.

"We don't give a rhino's ass, you understand?"

Blood drooled down Dom's chin onto his Led Zeppelin "Stairway to Heaven" T-shirt.

"Dom, he's a liar! A pathological liar! A sicko!"

Dom gaped at Ruby. She was mixed, part black or Caribbean with cocoa skin and green eyes like tiger marbles. Except for her freaky haircut, she was beautiful. Maybe the hair was a fashion statement or symptom of the disease.

"Tell him, you're not Edwin Ryan. Tell him, one true thing," she said.

"Who says I'm not? And if I happen to like the sound of Edwin Ryan,

I can change my name to whatever, even a symbol like that queer dude, Prince."

"Dom, he picked my mom up in a bar. My mom's not a slut. But he picked her up. She's a good person, too good. He appealed to her goodness. She wanted to help him but she made a mistake. Like you, Dom. When she tried to dump him, the mistake stuck around our house. His name isn't Edwin, it's Troy."

"Troy Mason?" Dom asked.

"He didn't have a dime. All he had was a bunch of bullshit stories. Every day he lied to us like he lied to you. My mother gave him her savings to get rid of him. He would have killed me if I hadn't shot him."

"You *shot* him?" Dom asked.

"Shut up, cunt! You stole my money, my gun, my car! You shot me in the knee! You're going down!" Troy's voice echoed through the metal box.

"Leave it alone," Quinn told Ruby.

"You're not Edwin Ryan. You couldn't be him in a million years."

"I believe I am Edwin Ryan."

"You don't believe anything," Ruby said. "That's what makes you evil."

Troy leapt from a folding chair, lunged at Ruby, and rammed her with his head. She rolled in a ball. Quinn rolled on top of her. Troy hopped back and charged again. When he contacted Quinn, he knocked the breath out of him.

Justice Jenkins sprang from the top of the tank, slammed Troy against the wall, and gripped his scrawny throat.

"You want to die today?" he asked coolly.

Scorn lingered on Troy's pretty face until the hand of one man and the air passage of the other reached the liminal threshold between breath and death.

"Answer before I snap your neck like a turkey wishbone."

"No," Troy croaked.

Snorri shone a flashlight into the tank where Quinn and Ruby were prone, nearly unconscious and Dom crouched down and bleeding.

"Get them out!" Jenkins ordered.

Two cadets helped Quinn and Dom up the steps and out of the tank. But Ruby refused to be touched.

Snorri motioned for the others to back off and let him try. He approached her gently. He promised not to hurt her. She tried to tell him to fuck off but couldn't find the strength. He explained that he was going to lift and sling her over his shoulder. He asked if that was okay. When Ruby didn't respond, he softly recited an Icelandic poem and proceeded. She was limp and silent as he carried her up the steps.

The rain fell through the open hatch of the tank into a shallow puddle that filled the center of the floor. Justice pressed his boot on Troy's chest.

"Who are you?" he asked, squinting his minuscule eyes. In Edwin Ryan he perceived an amoral man, a loose thread of Chaos, a scoundrel. Justice Jenkins used to be that man. "Who?" he pressed harder.

There were lots of answers to that question but Troy was weary. With a man like Jenkins, he had to play a different hand.

"Troy Mason, born and raised in Amarillo. Mechanic by trade, I been around, in and out."

"Who sent you?"

"Nobody," Troy said.

"Look at me!" Justice demanded.

Troy tried to find an aperture in the two points.

"If you don't want to volunteer, we got methods. Or we can improvise. Imagine, improvise, implement, that's the story of invention." Jenkins ticked off his fingers. "Water board, branding iron, stun gun, gibbet. Being a Texas boy, I bet you seen most of them." Justice kicked a solid cube. "Americans invented electro-torture. There's a battery right there, MADE IN USA."

"I swear," Troy muttered.

Justice Jenkins tapped Troy's face with the metal tip of his boot. "Good night," he said.

In the center of the clearing, he stripped down to his briefs. The cold needle-sharp raindrops pummeled him like sprays of fine gravel. Ice to fire. Drops ran down his head and neck and over his arms and legs. They stung his back and the scallop of flesh around his waist. He opened his mouth and swished the hard rain pellets with his tongue. He went to his knees and cupped his hands like a child. Every morning and every night, he came to Jesus, hoping his sins would be forgiven.

So far, that hadn't happened. He listened but heard nothing. He prayed and no one answered. Not only was he abandoned by God but now his wife and son had deserted him.

49

It was difficult for Snorri to sleep. The noises from the other boys disturbed him. Joab mumbled through the night, Shem wheezed. Even with earplugs, Snorri could hear them. He left the tent and crept beneath the large Douglas fir. Although the rain hammered away, he was dry under its web of branches and needles. Camp rules forbade tobacco and weed but rules were easy to ignore. For Snorri, it was a matter of pride. If you trusted yourself, rules weren't necessary. He took one toke and another followed.

While he smoked, he thought about Ruby. It had been six months since he'd touched a girl. The last was a weirdo who hung around the EK clubhouse. She meant nothing to him but Ruby electrified him. Her skin was silk, cream, fur, the softest things in the world. When he gazed into the darkness, her shapely physique and magenta lips appeared among the trees. Her eyes, he couldn't describe. Their color was like an imaginary sea or ancient scarab. And she was tough. She talked shit to the asshole. Tough and tender, sour and sweet. Lines of poetry flowed through him as he wrestled with his feelings.

She reminded him of Darneshia, his girlfriend in tenth grade. Darneshia was the only girl he'd ever loved. For three months, they loved in secret after school at his house when no one was home. Her twin brothers broke it up. They told him to stop messing with their African sister. They said they were descendants of a tribal king in Ghana who would never approve of white trash for Darneshia. If they caught him with her again, they threatened to brand him and cut off his nuts. When Darneshia told him she couldn't be his girlfriend, Snorri spray-painted *Fuck Niggers!* on a dozen STOP signs near her house. It caused a furor in the neighborhood and initiated a hate-crime investigation. Darneshia's brothers knew who did it but they left him alone.

Snorri reasoned that if ghetto boys in SE Seattle claimed princehood, so could he. He attached himself to the Nordic gods: Thor, Odin, Loki, Ullr. He combed the small section in the library on Scandinavian myth and folklore. He read the Icelandic Sagas.

Ullr is such a good archer and ski-runner
that no one can rival him.
Ullr is beautiful to look at as well and
he has all the characteristics of a warrior.

He found a genealogist who traced his mother's family with the surnames Voll, Kleve, Ross, and Breland back to villages in Norway and northern Scotland. She mailed him a stamped Certificate of White Nobility. When he turned eighteen, Peter changed his name to Snorri. His namesake was Snorri Sturluson, Icelandic historian, poet, military leader, and *skald* who chronicled the heroic wars of the Norsemen.

A year later, Snorri joined EK. EK members liked to discuss white lineage and Norse customs, raiding, honor killings, runes, and songs. There was an EK clubhouse but Snorri wasn't required to hang out there. He could be part and separate at the same time. Nobody minded if he came and went. EK promised that the American race wars were imminent. He hoped to kill Darneshia's brothers but the Crips beat him to it.

As he smoked, he listened to the percussive patter of rain. Thoughts raced through his mind. His mother was not well. She had mental problems. His two younger sisters had been sent to live with their aunt in Utah. He wished he could make them happy. That was his deepest wish but he'd already tried and failed. Now he didn't think it was possible. In the city, nothing seemed possible. He was only happy near rivers, mountains, trees. Rapturous and free of bullshit rules, bullshit school, bullshit government. He thought he might become a recluse and worship the deities of the Old World.

The trip to Patriot Park had been useful. It reinforced how much he hated camp mentality. He hated Christian platitudes. He'd grown up with them and heard enough. Except for Captain Eli, everyone else was stupid. Worse than stupid, they were barnyard animals under the domination of Commander Justice.

In the Sagas, Snorri read that Norsemen migrated to Iceland to escape the monarchy in Norway with its royal tithing and royal laws. In Iceland, the chieftains assembled once a year at the *Althing* to judge disputes and organize their governance. Snorri had visions of Thule and Viking ships. He believed he'd been born at the wrong time in history. In those times, it was easier for a man to know himself. Last year he saved a few hundred dollars. When he had a few hundred more, he planned to travel to Iceland to visit Gulfoss and the ruins of Snorri Sturluson's estate at Reykholt where he was murdered in 1241.

Snorri snuffed the smoldering joint on his tongue. As he started to return to his tent, Justice Jenkins appeared on top of the tank. He watched Justice walk to the center of the clearing. He watched him take off his clothes. Except for his briefs and the belted knife around his waist, he was naked. He lifted his chest and arched his back. He parted his lips to drink rain from the sky. Then he bowed on the ground.

Like a fucking pagan, Snorri thought. At that instant with his bow in hand, Justice Jenkins would have been a bulls-eye. A single arrow would have brought him down like a buck.

50

David had saved Hazel's child. He had honored his training and oath. The star around his neck reminded him a man is never judged by himself alone. He advised Hazel to rest in the tent and wait for a raft or jetboat to stop at Bargamin.

"Someone will take you and Lucas. You'll be able to contact the rangers. They'll help you get Lucas to a hospital." From his rocket box, he removed a few hundred dollars and handed them to Hazel. "For medicine or food, whatever you need," he said.

The fortune sifted between her fingers. She'd never seen a hundred dollars. She had no idea how people acquired money. At fourteen, she'd run away from her father's house with nothing. Shortly afterwards, Justice Jenkins married her. He'd taken care of her.

"Lucas got well," she said.

"He's better but you should find out what caused the fever. He should be tested."

"When you call the ranger station, tell them where we are," Kate said. "Help us save *my* Ruby."

Hazel searched for God's will inside her. It had directed her from camp. It had guided her to Dr. Tanner. Now she knew the doctor was a Jew like Jesus. A savior like Jesus. But next to God, Justice had always been in charge. Her loyalties divided. She weighed one against the other. Jenkins saved her, but David and Kate saved Lucas. She described the way to Jenkins's camp and suggested David remove his star.

They stuffed their packs with clothes and food. They wrapped the sleeping bags in plastic and strapped them to the bottom of the packs. They put on rain gear and left the tent for Hazel and Lucas. She followed them over the wooden bridge that crossed Bargamin Creek. Even after they were out of sight, they heard her.

"Thank you! Thank you!" she wept.

The swift putty-colored water roared between its banks, carrying sand, rock, sections of trees, debris, whirling and rushing to the river.

"You won't be able to reason with him," Kate said.

"I'll handle it," David said.

It was only on the river that he felt a semblance of certainty. Maybe it was the certainty of transience. There was a quote from Einstein he liked: *Living matter and clarity are opposites—they run away from one another.*

"And once we find her?"

"I don't know," Kate confessed.

"It couldn't have been easy."

"It didn't work for Ruby," she said.

Mistake after mistake. She never married a decent man to father Ruby. She wasn't strict about school. She'd isolated Ruby to protect her. It was easy to understand why Ruby hated Zamora. Isolation was a curse.

"When this nightmare is over, if you need me," David said. He hoped to make his mistakes up to Kate.

Kate couldn't speak about a future. There was no future until Ruby was beside her.

51

Inside his tepee, Captain Eli slept on a platform covered by a buffalo hide. A teenage woman and Goshen, their son, were next to him, also sleeping. Quinn and Dom lay on rugs on one side of the bed and Ruby on the other. The prisoners each had a fifty-pound ball-and-chain anchored to one leg and their arms tied behind their back. The ball-and-chains were antebellum relics that Eli stole from the Confederacy museum in Vicksburg.

Snorri glided into the tepee and over to Ruby. Once his eyes adjusted to the dark, he drank in her face, perfectly reposed as if she were marble. According to legend, her skin had been darkened to protect her from sun and her hair shorn as a sign of respect for she was the daughter of a Norn, one of the giantesses who sat at the foot of Yggdrasil. It was the Norn who had carried Snorri's fate in their hearts since he was born. Without the Norn to guide him, he would have died a violent death long ago.

He squatted beside Ruby. He laid his bow on the canvas floor of the tepee. A watchman cap was pulled over his head and brow. The silver pendant of Thor's Hammer was tucked inside his shirt. He'd removed his swastika earrings and leather wristbands. He wore long sleeves to cover his tattoos. He didn't want Ruby to think he was a Nazi fanatic. He was a poet-warrior like his namesake, both gentle and fierce.

"Awake! Awake!" he mutely mouthed the words.

Minutes passed. Ruby's eyelids fluttered. Her weight shifted. She called faintly for Quinn and shifted again. A minute more, her eyes widened with amazement at the sight of Snorri only inches away.

"Hush!" He motioned with his finger on his lips.

She felt his breath fanning her face. As she started to yell, he slapped a piece of duct tape over her mouth, scooped her up, slung the chain with the iron ball over his shoulder, and tucked his bow under his armpit. Soundlessly, he tiptoed out of the tepee into the wild rainy night.

Ruby struggled. However, struggle was painful and resistance futile. Her abductor was strong and determined. He was testing his strength, matching it to the expectations of the gods.

"I would never hurt you," he whispered.

She felt his eyes boring into her, eyes that would eat her if they could.

"I'm taking you away from Patriot bullshit Park."

She shook her head.

"You don't wanna go?"

The shaking increased.

"Don't be afraid of me."

Tears rolled down Ruby's face.

"Hush," he soothed. "You hiding already, I can tell. Hiding from scum, law, your family, I don't care. You and me, we can hide together from Jesus Jenkins. He won't ever find us. I swore an oath to Odin."

Snorri laid her under the Douglas fir where she would stay dry. He examined the chain around Ruby's ankle. He snuck back inside the tepee and stretched out in her spot. He watched and waited while his eyes adjusted to the cone of darkness. Maybe he could find the key.

Eli Jenkins opened his eyes. Something had disrupted his sleep. Something foreign had come on the premises. He listened closely. Raccoons occasionally wandered around. A moose once pulled down a clothesline. He retrieved the revolver under his pillow. He scanned the interior of the tepee: rugs, clothing, a rocking horse, the sleeping prisoners. Their youth touched him. He was touched by their fear. Like children, it was fear that made them compliant. Of the three, the girl was the least fearful. He especially liked the girl. It was girls who usually got him in trouble. He would try to be sensible. However, he couldn't promise Jesus or himself to behave. The girl reminded him too much of Lucille.

Eli listened for anything besides the usual noises of the forest and the sleeping restless bodies. He listened and dozed. Finally he slept.

Once Snorri heard Eli's even breathing, he crawled through the flap of the teepee. He went to Ruby and cut the ties around her hands. Then he picked her up with the ball-and-chain and sprinted through the woods to a fire road that went north away from camp, creek, and river.

After a mile, he rested. He laid Ruby down on a bed of duff. He was wet with rain and sweat, shivering, overheated, chilled. From a rock ledge, he removed a stash of water, crackers, a sweatshirt, sandals, arrows, and a flashlight.

"I'll take off the tape," he said, putting his forefinger to his lips. "If you swear. Swear?"

He detected a sparkle of trust in her eyes. He lifted the tape from her mouth. He offered her a drink. She took a swallow of water, then let out a piercing scream which ricocheted through the woods. It awakened both Jenkins brothers. Troy heard it too and groped for the steps in the tank.

"Joab, cocksucker, where the fuck are the steps?" Troy shouted.

Eli rose and walked outside. The rain had turned to light mist. Overhead a fraction of moon glimmered. Clouds danced the tarantella. The storm was nearly spent.

He checked inside Justice's tepee. "You hear that?"

"Screech owl," Justice said.

"Screech owl," Eli repeated and returned to bed.

Snorri replaced the tape. He retied Ruby's wrists. "When you no longer doubt me," he said.

She watched him towel his hair and change his shirt. She watched him study the sky. She listened to what sounded like prayers. She wasn't sure if he was stoned or deranged. When he finished his ritual, he picked her up again and walked purposefully northward, always north.

She looked for markers or signs but nothing stood out. On both sides of the fire road were trees. In the distance, more trees. She thought they'd probably get lost and starve. Snorri's canteen of water and food wouldn't last long. In a year or so, their skeletons would be discovered. Hunters or hikers, forest rangers clearing weeds, someone would find them and be horrified, especially by the ball-and-chain. That would make a sensational headline. They'd send out an impression of her teeth to a forensic dentist. Eventually she'd be identified by George Heller, DDS, in Santa Fe. He would verify the teeth belonged to Ruby Ryan from Zamora, New Mexico, who mysteriously disappeared in the Bitterroot Wilderness. Finally her mother would learn what happened to her. That made Ruby happy. "Closure," they called it. Kate would have closure. At least, there would be something to bury.

Ruby leaned back in Snorri's arms. She looked at the underside of his jaw, the deep dimple in his chin, the tattooed scroll around his throat. She didn't recognize the language. She picked out umlauts and letters dotted by rings. Sanskrit? Arabic? He was breathing heavily but his demeanor was calm. Except for an occasional glance at Ruby, he focused straight ahead.

When the road shifted south, his pace slowed. He stopped. He waved his flashlight at the edge of the brush. There was a two-foot cairn made of schist.

As Snorri stepped with Ruby into the rain-drenched forest, she remembered Justice Jenkins's words: *trade the devil for a witch.*

52

When Jenkins opened his eyes, Hazel was beside him. She wore a blue nylon poncho he'd never seen. Her hair was wet and disheveled. She looked thinner and the habitual frightened expression in her eyes was noticeably gone. Apparition or answered prayer, he wasn't sure.

Justice saw no child. He assumed Lucas was dead. His only son dead. It was Hazel's fault. She'd wrenched him from the circle of his father's love and protection. She'd exposed him to the storm. Justice turned away in disgust. When he looked again, she hadn't moved. He could see her eyes were also filled with blame. She blamed him.

"Where'd you leave him?" he growled.

"I didn't leave him, Mr. Jenkins," she said.

"Where's his body then?"

Hazel set her misshapen teeth on her lower lip. "He done got well. He got professional licensed help. Otherwise, he'd have died."

Justice cast her a look of disbelief. If only to prove her wrong, she sensed he wished Lucas was dead. But she wasn't wrong. Justice would be forced to admit she did the right thing.

"That's good," he sighed wearily. His son had come back to him like Isaac to Abraham, Joseph to Jacob. "But *where* is he?"

"He nearly died from fever but I found a doctor who saved him. The doctor got liquids in him. The doctor and Kate kept him alive. They stayed up all night. They saved our boy, Mr. Jenkins."

As Justice listened, he guessed the boy had died and his wife lost her mind.

"What doctor, Hazel?"

"They did it with Jesus guiding them, the doctor and Jesus. He's a Jew like Jesus."

"What you talking about?"

"Jesus and Dr. Tanner."

Justice twisted her hair.

"Maybe you didn't know about all that," she said, slipping out of reach.

"Where's my boy?" he demanded.

"Doctor got him, making sure his vital signs are good before he gives him back."

Hazel had followed Kate and David up Bargamin Creek and led them to the entrance of the camp. She left them with Lucas at the boulder. Against her husband's will, she had taken Lucas away and returned with her own will. She believed she could intervene for Ruby.

The storm had blown east. The day was clear and warm. On such days, Kate thought only good was possible. Sometimes weather was how she sorted out good from bad.

"Let's go in," David said.

They squeezed between the crevice of rock and followed the path, stepping across the runnels of rainwater. In the wind, the wet trees showered a thousand drops to the ground. The sound was lovely. Nature laughing. Another sign, Kate thought.

Hazel and Justice Jenkins were at the end of the clearing when Kate and David appeared, Lucas in David's arms.

Jenkins strode toward them, his eyes like sparks.

He shall baptize you with the Holy Ghost, and with fire: whose fan is in his hand, and he will thoroughly purge his floor, and gather his wheat into the garner.

Fear rippled through David. Justice Jenkins might prove too much for him. David was mostly reason and Jenkins was reason's opposite. Madness, he supposed. A man possessed.

He responded with a prayer from his youth.

Deliver me, O Lord, from the evil man: preserve me from the violent man; which imagine mischiefs in their heart: continually are they gathered together for war.

Jenkins's lips curled.

My flesh and my heart faileth; But God is the rock of my heart and my portion for ever.

"We've brought back your son," David said.

Justice stopped only inches away. "He's all right then?"

"We're watching him. His breathing isn't normal yet."

"His mother can tend him," Jenkins said, reaching for the child.

"We haven't come to bother your people here." David held onto Lucas. "We've come to take Ruby and her cousin home."

"They trespassed."

"We've all trespassed," David said.

"Where are they?" Kate cried.

"Let them go, Justice," Hazel demanded.

Kate took David's arm. They stood bonded with Jenkins's child.

Justice Jenkins was confounded. He had again lost control. Within twenty-four hours, a third pair of strangers had invaded Patriot Park. Mongrels, charlatans, perverts, Jews, they'd poisoned Hazel.

David would have to be canny but he was tired. Jenkins had weapons and men, Ruby and Quinn. However, he had Lucas. He spoke.

> *The Lord said to Moses, 'Yet one plague more I will bring upon Pharaoh and upon Egypt; afterwards he will let you go hence; when he lets you go, he will drive you away completely.'*

He watched Jenkins's face, gambling he would understand the threat of the last plague. David held Lucas in the barter. To get his son, Jenkins would have to barter too.

Across the clearing, a white-haired man emerged from a tepee. A capote, cut and sewn from a Pendleton blanket, was thrown over his shoulders. He carried a staff. He was barefoot, his instep bandaged. He limped toward them. He nodded to his brother. He smiled at Lucas and Hazel.

"They come for Ruby and the boy," Justice said.

Eli jerked his head toward the tepee. "Ruby's gone."

53

The rain had stopped. Silver clouds tumbled in the sky around the setting moon. When they reached his cave, it was nearing the end of night. Snorri removed the brush piled outside the entrance. He sniffed around. He checked his altar, a slab of pink granite piled with a collection of rocks, snake skins, a hawk wing, tortoise shell, and skull of a raccoon. Around the altar were twenty storm candles. He lit them all. In the shallow fire pit, he placed kindling and a small cedar branch, enough fire to remove the chill.

"Welcome!" he said, lifting Ruby over the threshold like a groom.

It was warm with smells of melting wax, aromatic smoke, sprigs of smoldering sage.

"Did you make this?" Her eyes widened with wonder at the dancing shadows, the stumps for tables and seats, the cartons of water and food.

Since Snorri arrived at Patriot Park, he'd explored the mountains, looking for a hideaway retreat. Late at night when he wouldn't be missed, he liberated supplies from camp and transported them up the mountain.

"It's sacred," he said shyly.

"Magical," she said. Away from the Jenkinses and other cadets, Snorri was different. Not hard-core but soft and tender. "Will you stay here long?"

"As long as *you* want," he said.

"Me?" Ruby was astonished. "What do I have to do with it?"

He closed her hands inside his. He wanted to tell her she was the daughter of the Norn who had carried his fate in her heart since birth. But he had to choose his words carefully and prepare her slowly.

"The story is long," he said. "It's too late to begin now. When we wake up, it'll be sunny and hot. After breakfast, I'll show you the creek where we can swim."

"I can't swim with this," Ruby wiggled her foot.

"Don't worry," he said.

What was left of night and most of morning, they slept. Ruby dreamed she was in a passageway made of concrete blocks, stories high and roofless so she could see sky and treetops. In the dream, her father came to her. Not a boy or teenage athlete or the soldier she'd studied in photos but an old man. "Help, daddy!" Staring back were Edwin Ryan's eyes that said there was no help.

Hours later when they awoke, the day was as Snorri predicted. The entrance to the cave was flooded with light. Snorri sang a song in an archaic language. He cut wedges of apples and stirred dry milk and water into a bowl of cereal. He sang well, Ruby thought. His voice was beautiful.

"One bowl, two spoons," he said.

"Where'd you learn to cook?" she laughed.

"Hey, I worked as a cook."

"Like where you unwrap a patty and slap it on a grill cook?"

"You tasted better?" he asked, crunching the cornflakes.

Ruby took a spoonful. "Awesome!"

"I told you," he said.

"Better than mom's homemade granola and my mom makes the best granola on the mountain."

"You got a mom?" Snorri was surprised.

"Of course, dodo! If you born, you got a mom. But no problem if you tell me you flew in from another planet, I believe you."

"But are you still in contact with your mom?"

Ruby touched her heart. "My mom and I, we're connected."

"Where's your mom now?"

"Home in New Mexico, worrying about me. Sometimes I dream she died of worry."

"What's she like, your mom? You look like her?"

"She's a white girl," Ruby laughed.

"Really white?" Snorri liked that.

"Except she's Jewish."

"That's not really white," he said. "That's *pretend* white."

Snorri dug inside a carton, looking for a rectangular box. He lifted the lid and removed an Extreme Survival knife with a six-inch cutting blade and chainsaw-style teeth. He set it against the chain on Ruby's ankle.

"They got a millennium stockpile back there at f'ing Patriot Park," he said. "Excuse my f'ing language but they never opened half of it. We could live here for years on what they got."

"Don't cut me!"

"I'd never hurt you," he said, taking a corner of his shirt and wedging it between the iron links and her ankle. "Justice is a f'ing sadist, you know that? Excuse my language, but ball-and-chain, he's out of his mind! Bringing a tank into the forest, it's a sacrilege!"

"He's a Nazi."

"Nazis ain't all you think," Snorri said.

"Nazis killed millions, that's what I know, Jews, gypsies, gay people, Jehovah Witness, millions."

"Maybe, maybe not," Snorri said. He moved the blade evenly across the chain. "People say it's a lie. Jews made it up to get money."

"That's really ignorant."

"Nazis got a few bad parts," he conceded. "I give you that much. But Christians? They really fucked up. Excuse my language but they killed way more people than Nazis. They killed almost all the people in the New World. Two continents, three with Australia. So many millions, nobody can count them."

Ruby shrugged. She knew about the tragedy of Native Americans. They lived down the road.

"My mom's not Jewish anymore. She's Indian and Buddhist."

"If you born Jew or colored or gook, you don't just forget it."

"My mom really works at forgetting. She sits and meditates to empty her mind. She goes into the mountains and collects plants for medicine. She beads and weaves Indian baskets. My mom's so strange, she put my umbilical cord in a beaded pouch."

"No way!" Snorri laughed.

"When I turn eighteen, she told me I can have the pouch and do whatever I want. Like it's my graduation present!"

"I like her," Snorri said.

Ruby looked doubtful. "Sometimes she kills a chicken but other than that, she's way peaceful. Too peaceful if you ask me. She tells peace stories. Like what happened when a holy man told his disciples to take a duck and kill it where no one could see."

Snorri stopped moving the blade. "And what happened?"

"One killed the duck in an alley. The other wandered around for days. When he came back, the duck was alive. He told his teacher that everywhere he went, the duck could see."

"Peaceful is what I wanna be," Snorri said. "That's why I brought us here. Maybe you see moose or bears or wolves but nothing like vicious humans."

The saw-teeth on the knife worked well but Snorri's fingers cramped. He had to stop and stretch his fingers.

"Nazis want everyone to be white and perfect," Ruby said. "If you're brown or black or mixed, you're already fucked up. Nazis hate what I am."

"I'm not a hater, Ruby. Sometimes I get angry about the fucked-up world but I'm not a hater. What I know is you can't love everybody. You got to love your family first, right? You love your ancestry because that's family. *Roots* is like that for you. It's a lot of people, thousands if you do the genealogy. I did that. I found out about my origins. But today most people are either stupid or crazy. I don't see any reason to love them."

"My mom says she loves everybody, even scumbags. But I think it's wishful thinking. She wants to love everybody but no one can do it. Maybe the Dalai Lama can do it. You know about him?"

"I'm over people," Snorri said. "People make me think I'm crazy. Being outdoors doesn't do that. When I go somewhere like here, everything is perfect, even me. My mom is a sicko. It runs in my family. Do I look pure white or something else?"

Except for his forehead and cheeks where the skin had peeled raw from sunburn, Snorri's smooth baby face was the color of safflower oil, his eyes dark brown and traced with lines of gold, his hair and eyebrows black, his teeth yellow like his skin.

"Not so white," she said.

"When you have a chance to hear the stories, you'll understand how it fits together. Like you and me, we fit together."

The iron chain was crumbling. Five, nine, fifteen more strokes of the blade and the chain fell off Ruby's leg. She jumped up and kept jumping as high as she could.

"Fit together for what?" she laughed hysterically.

"To love," Snorri confessed. "Because I'm not a hater, Ruby. All I wanna do is love."

"I think I'm a hater," she said.

"You hate me?"

"I don't know," she said.

Ruby saw how much Snorri wanted her to love him. No one as handsome as Snorri had ever loved her. But his eyes were scary. He was old, almost twenty-five, and a born-again Nazi. On the positive side, he treated her gently. He recited poetry. She liked that he was a pagan and believed she was the daughter of a goddess. For certain, she didn't want to die a virgin. That was in his favor.

He kissed her on the neck. His lips drifted to her mouth. They kissed and after they stopped, breathless and hungry for more, Snorri whispered, "I wanna start my own race."

54

"Where are they?" David asked.

"Anywhere," Eli said.

"I warned you about them boys, bro," Justice chuckled.

"I bet somebody knows where they are," David said.

"What about Quinn?" Kate shouted, "Quinn!"

"No shouting!" Justice reprimanded.

Quinn hopped to the flap of the tepee. He peeked through the opening with disbelief.

"Aunt Kate!" he whooped.

Behind Quinn stood another young man, sleepy and disoriented. Both had a ball-and-chain.

"You know her?" Dom asked.

"Ruby's gone, Aunt Kate," Quinn gulped.

"Does Ruby have one of those?" David stared at the shackles.

"How could she go?" Kate asked.

"Where, that would be my question," Eli said.

A half dozen young men in camouflage pants, barefoot and bare-topped with shaved heads and multiple tattoos, stumbled into the clearing. The camp's women and children followed. When they saw Lucas and Hazel, they sang, "Hallelujah!"

"Is he dead?" Goshen tugged on David's jeans.

"He's sick," the doctor warned.

"You making him sicker," Justice said.

"He needs his mother," Eli added.

"Where's Ruby?" David's eyes circled the group.

"She gone?" Hazel's sister asked.

"With Snorri," Eli confirmed.

"Maybe to the river," Shem said.

"We just came from the river," Kate said.

"He's a pagan," Justice commented.

"What's that mean?" David asked.

"He worships trees and mountains. He don't want to go back to civilization. That's where the river goes."

"He likes it up here," Eli said.

"Has he got somewhere to go?" Kate asked.

"The girl's gone?" Joab asked.

"Kidnapped," Shem said.

"Lots of places to go," Justice speculated.

"But is there a particular place?" David insisted. "Or did they randomly go off?"

"Nothing random about Snorri," Eli said.

"Can someone tell me *where*?" David tried to control himself. "Ruby's mother and I drove a thousand miles to find her. We followed them down the river. We don't intend to make trouble. All we want is to take them home."

"I wanna go," Dom said.

"You don't know them, son," Justice said. "You don't know anything about them, whether they speak truth or tell devil lies. Didn't you learn your lesson about taking off with strangers? Now you want to go off with them?"

"Yes, sir," Dom said decisively.

"But you never met them."

"It's a free country, sir."

"Too free if you asking me," Justice grunted.

"What's it take to find them?" David asked.

"Time," Eli murmured.

"We got a pagan loose in the woods," Justice said. "You brought him over here. I let him stay because of your word. Now he's taken off with his mulatto concubine. What happens when he decides to sabotage us?"

"I realize what I heard last night," Eli said.

"You heard an owl."

"I heard a girl scream."

"Ruby scream?" Kate cried.

"Bastard could bring the law down in a minute."

"What would he want with law?" Eli turned to Snorri's friends, Philly and Thorn. "Right, boys?"

"To get back at us," Justice said. "To get back at Jesus. All his gods against the One God. He got no use for Christian goodness. Anything he do to hurt us, that's cause for pagan celebration. Right, boys?"

"What about money?" David asked.

"Money don't buy much here," Justice said. "Maybe a can of beans."

Philly lit up. "How much?"

"You a guide?"

"What's that mean?" Philly asked.

"If you know where Snorri went and can take us there, I'll pay you."

"How much?"

"Thousand dollars!"

"David!" Kate protested.

"Cash?" Philly asked.

"Good as cash," David said. "Worth more on the street."

"You plan to fight pagans?" Justice whistled through his teeth.

"I don't plan to fight anyone."

"You might want to reconsider," Eli cautioned.

"Doc, you figure you want the same thing as Snorri. You want Ruby and he got Ruby. I want Lucas and you holding Lucas. But Snorri, he's a crooked soul. Better to bargain with Christians. You give me Lucas, I'll help you find the girl."

Kate lifted Lucas from David's arms. She handed him to Jenkins. Justice pinched and patted his little son. "Thank you, Missus Ryan."

"We still need a guide."

"What product?" Philly asked.

David rubbed the tips of his fingers with his thumb.

"No, shit," Philly said.

"Top-grade shit."

"Like how much?"

"Like enough," David promised.

55

Justice didn't like the Jew doctor but he trusted Kate. Her maternal pain touched him. It recalled his mother's grief after their youngest brother, Vernon, was killed in prison. Justice knew any generosity he showed Kate would impress Hazel. He desperately needed Hazel back on his side.

Within a half hour, the rescue party was organized. Absalom, Quinn, and Dom would come with them up the mountain. The other cadets would stay with Shem. In case of further incidents, they had instructions. As for Troy Mason, he was to be fed and left in the tank.

Justice Jenkins delivered his blessing for their departure.

And I saw no temple in the city, for its temple is the Lord God the Almighty and the Lamb. And the city has no need of sun or moon to shine upon it, for the glory of God is its light, and its lamp is the Lamb. We ask Your Help to light our way, to find Ruby Ryan healthy and whole, and to place her back in the safekeeping of her mother and Thee. Amen.

Kate shut her eyes. She laced her fingers together on her chest. She prayed.

They headed north, according to Philly, following the fire road that Snorri had followed the night before. Philly knew part of the way. On two occasions, he'd helped Snorri carry supplies.

At first Philly had qualms, especially since he would profit. Profiting at the expense of his friend was a betrayal. That's what his conscience told him. But Philly was able to rationalize his decision. It was Snorri who betrayed EK. Snorri was a traitor to the white race. If Philly got a chance to kill him, he decided it would be okay.

The road climbed steadily into the mountains bordered on both sides by forest, outcrops of rock, talus slopes, and creeks full from recent rains.

"How far?" David asked.

He depended on calculations. No doctor took risks without knowing odds. Most of his life, he'd had an exit strategy. That's what the drugs were. But here, he had nothing to play. He couldn't think of one move to put himself on top. He and Kate were at the mercy of two maniacs, Justice and Eli Jenkins.

Philly wasn't sure about distance. He'd only walked in the dark and Snorri kept them going at a brutal pace. The increase in elevation, the heat of early afternoon, everyone's general fatigue made the going slow.

"Things will work out," David said to Kate. He wanted to lean on her faith. "Isn't that your creed?"

"They *will* work out," she replied, "but not necessarily well." Kate had faith but she wasn't a fool.

"Feels like ambush territory," Justice said, glancing into the dense thickets.

"No way he knows we coming," Philly said.

"He might," Eli said.

"Like who gives a fuck if he took off with a nigger girl?"

Kate spat in Philly's face. "Nigger girl is my baby!"

"You keep her in line." Justice pointed to David. "And I'll take care of mine."

Kate squatted on the ground, her head against her knees.

"How far, Philly?" David called.

Philly didn't answer. He hated these people.

"It can't be much farther," Eli said. He knew the mountains. A cave near a stream, he'd seen such a place.

David sat beside Kate. He held her hand. "Let the others go on," he said. They would catch up.

When the fire road veered south, Philly remembered the turn on a small path. Most of all, he remembered the cairn.

Snorri had dismantled the cairn but scattered along the path were a number of uniform rocks. Nearby was trampled foliage and a patch of mud with footprints.

"This is it." Philly was certain.

They convened on how to approach Snorri. They decided Eli should reconnoiter with Absalom and come back to report.

Eli checked his shotgun. He adjusted his Stetson. Absalom, dressed in a camouflage jumpsuit and camouflage cap, carried his nine-inch steel throwing knives. "Black Widow" knives, according to the catalog. For days he'd done almost nothing but practice. He could hit fifteen consecutive bulls-eyes.

"You think he's got a gun?" Justice asked.

"He plans to kill what he eats," Philly said. "I guess it ain't bare-handed."

"He's got his bow, " Eli added. "That's how he kills."

"Whose fault is that?" Justice asked.

Eli had fallen under the spell of pagan boys, which threatened to derail two years of the brothers' work.

"I'd like to go," Quinn offered.

Justice handed him a whistle.

"Go," he said. "Otherwise she'll run away like a rabbit, chain and all. Then we stuck hunting her down. You find trouble you can't handle, blow."

They entered the forest. After a few seconds, they disappeared.

"Trees just swallow them up," Justice said.

They moved stealthily, putting weight on their heels and stepping carefully along the trail where Snorri had dragged his cartons and tree stumps. As they walked, the silence expanded. An unearthly silence from the mountains and the ground. Even the birds were quiet, the wind still, the sky faded like stone-washed denim. By early evening, it would rain again.

When Eli saw signs of camp, he raised his hand. Snorri was not in sight. But Ruby was a few yards away, seated on a log, her outstretched legs free of impediments, her chin propped inside her palm, her elbows on her knees, her eyes cast down.

Eli prompted Quinn to step forward.

"Ruby," Quinn whispered.

Ruby raised her face, her eyes red and swollen.

"You okay?" he asked, moving toward her and kneeling in the mud.

"I don't know what I am."

That sounded right. That sounded sane.

"It's almost over," Quinn said.

"Is it?"

"I promise," he assured her. "We came to find you. Your mom and David Tanner are here. We all came."

"Mom!"

"They followed the river."

Eli stepped inside the circle of firs beside the cave. "Where's Snorri?"

Ruby's face contorted. "In there."

Snorri lay on a bed of pine straw, dressed in a blood-stained white robe, the silver necklace with the finely wrought pendant of Thor's Hammer framing his neck.

"What the hell!" Eli tried to find a pulse.

Ruby shook her head.

After breakfast they walked through the woods to the sparkling creek. They splashed like children in the chilly water with the hot sun on their backs. They sat on the bank, drying themselves. Ruby closed her eyes and listened to Snorri recite poetry about Norse gods and warriors. He told her about the ancient times of the Sagas when there were no kings, only chieftains. Snorri wanted to travel to Iceland. With Ruby, he hoped. Maybe they would move there and live next to a fjord.

When he asked Ruby if she loved him, she said she didn't know him. He told her their fate was entwined at the foot of Yggdrasil.

"That's only a story in your head," she said.

Snorri left her beside the creek. He thrashed his way through the woods. He yelled and cursed. Ruby plugged her ears so she wouldn't have to listen. When she returned to the cave, he was already there, dressed in white and lying on the pine straw bier. On the front of his robe, he'd written her name R-U-B-Y and N-O-R-N in blood.

She sat beside him. She held a bowl of water to his lips. She stroked his hands.

"Speak to me," she begged him.

56

For minutes Kate and Ruby stood pressed together, melding into one entity, one bloodstream, two hearts, one beat. Mother and child.

The return to camp was slow. The men took turns carrying Snorri. Two at a time on either side, they carried him under his armpits. His thigh was badly cut, his ankle sprained or broken. When they reached Patriot Park, they rested and ate. David cleaned Snorri's cut and splinted his ankle. They stayed through the rainy evening and wet night.

At dawn they gathered their things. Kate and David bid an emotional farewell to Hazel and Lucas. Abandoning Hazel to life with Justice Jenkins felt like a crime but Hazel would have called it "God's will."

Snorri hobbled between Dom and Quinn, his ankle blue and three times its normal size. David Tanner's painkillers weren't strong enough to mask the pain. But on the raft was a pharmacopeia of drugs, including morphine. As soon as they reached the river, David promised Snorri a shot.

From Patriot Park they climbed the path and passed through the split in the boulder, traversed the fire road, and wended their way beside Bargamin Creek back to the river where the canyon opened to the Main Fork of the Salmon, sometimes called River of No Return.

Around them, shadows hovered in the gray light. An assembly of creatures moving toward the river, creeping to the beach, scuttling on rocks, swooping overhead, splashing and diving, stepping to the water's edge, commencing their discourse, and filling the prelapsarian air with creature speech. Sunrise flamed on the ridges and voluminous clouds sailed by like caravels, setting out to sea.

In elementary Italian, David tried to sing, "*Pace, pace, mio Dio.*" His voice rising and falling with his huge feelings for it looked exactly like the beginning or end of the world.

Quinn pushed the raft away from shore into the shallows, steadying it as Kate, Ruby, and Dom with Snorri leaning across his back, waded into the water and climbed aboard. David untied the mooring ropes, shoved the raft toward the current, and hopped into the stern.

Once again, they were heading west toward the confluence of the Salmon with the Snake, toward Oregon and the mighty Columbia, on to the great Pacific Ocean. Out of nearly nowhere into somewhere, back to the human world.

EPILOGUE

Kate's Dodge Power Wagon waited for them in Riggins where a driver from Salmon had left it with her keys under the floor mat. From Riggins, they drove to Grangeville and the ER where Snorri's cut was stitched and his ankle set in a cast. David left him with four hundred dollars and painkillers.

Snorri apologized for scaring Ruby. He never intended to hurt himself, he said. He only wanted to test her love. He was sure he wouldn't return to Seattle. He thought he might head south to Los Angeles and become an actor. He asked Ruby if she minded if he wrote her.

At the Grangeville police department, Dominic and Quinn filed complaints against Troy Mason and the Jenkins brothers. Mason was wanted in New Mexico on suspicion of murder and eight counts of fraud. He had outstanding warrants in Texas, Florida, Hawaii, and California. Quinn identified the spot on a topo map where Mason was last seen inside an M4A2 Sherman tank approximately four miles northwest of the juncture of the Salmon River's Main Fork and Bargamin Creek.

FBI agents arrived from Boise. They interviewed all parties about The Adolph Brotherhood, otherwise known as TAB, the brainchild of the Jenkins brothers. In its recruitment literature, TAB claimed credit for assaults on African exchange students in Nevada, death threats to rabbis in Idaho and Oregon, and arson activities at black churches and migrant farm worker camps in California. Since the 1995 bombing of the federal building in Oklahoma City, the Jenkinses had been under surveillance. Kidnapping charges were filed against Justice Jenkins by the parents of fourteen-year-old Hazel Alcock and later dropped. That same year, TAB was the subject of a Southern Poverty Law Center investigation, which included interviews with Hazel's parents. Occasionally, the Jenkinses' uncle, Henry Fleet, sold information on TAB activities to the FBI and ATF.

Marnie Bass arrived in Boise and drove to Grangeville. She invited everyone back to the homestead in Salmon for a few days of rest, including Dom Gambolli.

Jenkins and his entourage disappeared quickly. Eli hurried to his small ranch near Colorado Springs, Justice to Sacramento. Hazel's faith in divine providence had been strengthened and the circle of Jesus's protection expanded to include Jews and colored people. She had two secrets she intended to keep from her husband: three hundred dollars and the telephone number of the clinic in Zamora.

The National Park Service raided Patriot Park and found it empty of human habitation except for Troy Mason. They towed out the tank. They removed the trash and supplies. Troy was taken into custody and airlifted by police helicopter from the Lazy OK to Grangeville.

In Zamora, Elaine Beasley prepared her letter of resignation effective upon Dr. Tanner's return.

After a half-hearted attempt at suicide, August was now on anti-depressants and under psychiatric care.

Over two weeks had passed since the night Hector Trujillo found Troy Mason shot in the knee and Ruby Ryan vanished. The Spanish farmers were gathered on Zamora's only blacktop road. Hector stood beside his brothers, cousins, an old uncle, and several lifelong friends. They were waiting for Dr. Tanner, Kate, and Ruby, expected to arrive at sunset, the high desert's most beautiful moment.

Hector had aired and tidied both households, stocked each larder with milk, tortillas, coffee, and homemade goat cheese. Marie Luisa had watered Dr. Tanner's roses and fed Kate Ryan's chickens. In addition, David had insisted that his opera tickets not go wasted. Hector took his wife to hear Verdi's *La Forza del Destino*, which he later told Dr. Tanner was even greater than their wedding night.

ABOUT THE AUTHOR

Summer Brenner was raised in Georgia and migrated west, first to New Mexico and eventually to Northern California, where she has been a longtime resident. She has published a dozen books of poetry, fiction, and novels for youth. Her works include the noir thriller from PM Press *I-5, A Novel of Crime, Transport, and Sex* (selected by Los Angeles Mystery Bookstore as a Top Ten Book of 2009), and from PM Press/Reach And Teach, *Ivy, Homeless in San Francisco* (winner of 2011 Children's Literary Classics and Moonbeam awards).

ABOUT PM PRESS

PM Press was founded at the end of 2007 by a small collection of folks with decades of publishing, media, and organizing experience. PM Press co-conspirators have published and distributed hundreds of books, pamphlets, CDs, and DVDs. Members of PM have founded enduring book fairs, spearheaded victorious tenant organizing campaigns, and worked closely with bookstores, academic conferences, and even rock bands to deliver political and challenging ideas to all walks of life. We're old enough to know what we're doing and young enough to know what's at stake.

We seek to create radical and stimulating fiction and non-fiction books, pamphlets, T-shirts, visual and audio materials to entertain, educate and inspire you. We aim to distribute these through every available channel with every available technology — whether that means you are seeing anarchist classics at our bookfair stalls; reading our latest vegan cookbook at the café; downloading geeky fiction e-books; or digging new music and timely videos from our website.

PM Press is always on the lookout for talented and skilled volunteers, artists, activists and writers to work with. If you have a great idea for a project or can contribute in some way, please get in touch.

PM Press
PO Box 23912
Oakland, CA 94623
www.pmpress.org

FRIENDS OF PM PRESS

These are indisputably momentous times—the financial system is melting down globally and the Empire is stumbling. Now more than ever there is a vital need for radical ideas.

In the four years since its founding—and on a mere shoestring—PM Press has risen to the formidable challenge of publishing and distributing knowledge and entertainment for the struggles ahead. With over 175 releases to date, we have published an impressive and stimulating array of literature, art, music, politics, and culture. Using every available medium, we've succeeded in connecting those hungry for ideas and information to those putting them into practice.

Friends of PM allows you to directly help impact, amplify, and revitalize the discourse and actions of radical writers, filmmakers, and artists. It provides us with a stable foundation from which we can build upon our early successes and provides a much-needed subsidy for the materials that can't necessarily pay their own way. You can help make that happen—and receive every new title automatically delivered to your door once a month—by joining as a Friend of PM Press. And, we'll throw in a free T-shirt when you sign up.

Here are your options:

- **$25 a month** Get all books and pamphlets plus 50% discount on all webstore purchases

- **$40 a month** Get all PM Press releases (including CDs and DVDs) plus 50% discount on all webstore purchases

- **$100 a month** Superstar—Everything plus PM merchandise, free downloads, and 50% discount on all webstore purchases

For those who can't afford $25 or more a month, we're introducing **Sustainer Rates** at $15, $10 and $5. Sustainers get a free PM Press T-shirt and a 50% discount on all purchases from our website.

Your Visa or Mastercard will be billed once a month, until you tell us to stop. Or until our efforts succeed in bringing the revolution around. Or the financial meltdown of Capital makes plastic redundant. Whichever comes first.

I-5

A Novel of Crime, Transport, and Sex

Summer Brenner

ISBN: 978-1-60486-019-1
$15.95 200 pages

A novel of crime, transport, and sex, *I-5* tells the brutal story of Anya and her journey north from Los Angeles to Oakland on the interstate that bisects the Central Valley of California. Someone has lied to Anya and because of these lies, she is kept under lock and key, used to service men, and indebted for the privilege. In exchange, she lives in America. "Would she rather be fucking a dog . . . or living like a dog?" In Anya's world, it's a reasonable question. It's a macabre journey up the interstate: a drop-off at Denny's, a patch of tule fog, a visit to a "correctional facility," a rendezvous with an organ grinder, and a fiery entry into Oakland. Only one last task stands between Anya and the freedom promised when she was lured away from Russia.

VOTED TOP TEN BOOKS OF 2009 — Los Angeles Mystery Bookstore

TOP 50 BOOKS OF THE DECADE — BSC Review

". . . it has a quality very rare in literature: a subtle, dark humor that's only perceivable when one goes deep into the heart of this world's absurd tragedy, or tragic absurdity."
— R. Crumb

"In I-5, Summer Brenner deals with the onerous and gruesome subject of sex trafficking calmly and forcefully, making the reader feel the pain of its victims. The trick to forging a successful narrative is always in the details, and I-5 provides them in abundance. This book bleeds truth—after you finish it, the blood will be on your hands."
— Barry Gifford, poet, screenwriter, novelist, author of *Wild at Heart*

". . . hard-boiled feminist thriller . . . without a superfluous word, it's a big chase, practically a movie on the page."
— Ned Sublette, author of *Cuba and Its Music* and *The Year Before the Flood: A Story of New Orleans*

"Anya is a wonderful, believable heroine, her tragic tale told from the inside out, without a shred of sentimental pity, which makes it all the stronger."
— Denise Hamilton, editor of *Los Angeles Noir* and author of the *LA Times* bestseller *The Last Embrace*

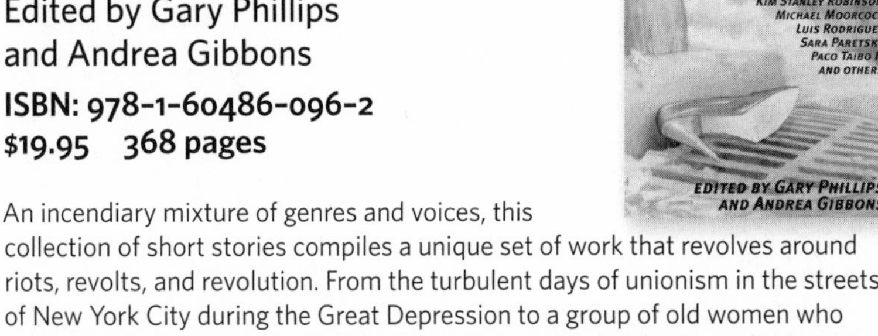

Send My Love and a Molotov Cocktail: Stories of Crime, Love and Rebellion

Edited by Gary Phillips
and Andrea Gibbons

ISBN: 978-1-60486-096-2
$19.95 368 pages

An incendiary mixture of genres and voices, this collection of short stories compiles a unique set of work that revolves around riots, revolts, and revolution. From the turbulent days of unionism in the streets of New York City during the Great Depression to a group of old women who meet at their local café to plan a radical act that will change the world forever, these original and once out-of-print stories capture the various ways people rise up to challenge the status quo and change up the relationships of power. Ideal for any fan of noir, science fiction, and revolution and mayhem, this collection includes works from Sara Paretsky, Paco Ignacio Taibo II, Cory Doctorow, Kim Stanley Robinson, and Summer Brenner.

Full list of contributors:

Summer Brenner
Rick Dakan
Barry Graham
Penny Mickelbury
Gary Phillips
Luis Rodriguez
Benjamin Whitmer
Michael Moorcock
Larry Fondation
Cory Doctorow
Andrea Gibbons
John A. Imani
Sara Paretsky
Kim Stanley Robinson
Paco Ignacio Taibo II
Ken Wishnia
Michael Skeet
Tim Wohlforth

Ivy, Homeless in San Francisco

Summer Brenner
with illustrations by Brian Bowes

ISBN: 978-1-60486-317-8
$15.00 176 pages

In this empathetic tale of hope, understanding, and the importance of family, young readers confront the difficult issues of poverty and the hardships of homelessness. Its inspiring young heroine is Ivy, who finds herself homeless on the streets of San Francisco when she and her father, Poppy, are evicted from their artist loft.

Struggling to survive day to day, Ivy and Poppy befriend a dog who leads them to the ramshackle home of octogenarian siblings, Eugenia and Oscar Orr. This marks the start of a series of desperate and joyful adventures that blend a spoonful of Charles Dickens' *Oliver Twist* with a dash of Armistead Maupin's *Tales of the City* and a few pinches of the *Adventures of Lassie*. Ivy's tale will appeal to young readers and adults, providing much material for discussion between generations.

Recipient of the Children's Literary Classics and MOONBEAM awards

"Ivy *is an engaging, educational experience, with emotional range, density of characters, a cinematic visual imagination, and a heroine wild at heart. We have a lot to learn about homelessness, and Summer Brenner's saga of fractured family and redeeming friendship takes us deep inside the experience, while agitating our broader concern with social justice. All this in a lucid, poetic prose. She not only will get young people to read but make them want to write as well."*
—John Broughton, associate professor of psychology & education, Teachers College, Columbia University

"Ivy *is a story of homelessness. It is full of risk and tenderness, pain and insight all mixed with fear and hope. Author Summer Brenner engages readers by setting a course for a young girl and her father that requires connection and kindness in an uneasy world. Genuine characters tell the tale that is at once prickly and gentle. Readers will gain a picture of what over 1.5 million children in the US experienced this year.* Ivy *is a lovely book on a tough condition."*
—Lyn Palme, library specialist, Contra Costa County, CA

with PM Press

A Moment of Doubt

Jim Nisbet

ISBN: 978-1-60486-307-9
$13.95 144 pages

A Moment of Doubt is at turns hilarious, thrilling and obscene. Jim Nisbet's novella is ripped from the zeitgeist of the 80s, and set in a sex-drenched San Francisco, where the computer becomes the protagonist's co-conspirator and both writer and machine seem to threaten the written word itself. The City as whore provides a backdrop oozing with drugs, poets and danger. Nisbet has written a mad-cap meditation on the angst of a writer caught in a world where the rent is due, new technology offers up illicit ways to produce the latest bestseller, and the detective and other characters of the imagination might just sidle up to the bar and buy you a drink in real life. The world of *A Moment of Doubt* is the world of phone sex, bars and bordellos, AIDS and the lure of hacking. Coming up against the rules of the game—the detective genre itself, has never been such a nasty and gender defying challenge.

Plus: An interview with Jim Nisbet, who is "Still too little read in the United States, it's a joy for us that Nisbet has been recognized here . . ." *Regards: Le Mouvement des Idées*

"He is as weird as the world. And for some readers, that's a quality to cherish. It's as if Nisbet inhabited and wrote from a world right next to ours, only weirder."
— Rick Kleffel, bookotron.com

"Missing any book by Nisbet should be considered a crime in all 50 states and maybe against humanity."
— Bill Ott, *Booklist*

"With Nisbet, you know you can expect anything and you're never disappointed."
— *Le Figaro*

"Jim Nisbet is a poet . . . [who] resembles no other crime fiction writer. He mixes the irony of Dantesque situations with lyric narration, and achieves a luxuriant cocktail that truly leaves the reader breathless."
— *Drood's Review of Mysteries*

with PM Press

Low Bite

Sin Soracco

ISBN: 978-1-60486-226-3
$14.95 144 pages

Low Bite Sin Soracco's prison novel about survival, dignity, friendship and insubordination. The view from inside a women's prison isn't a pretty one, and Morgan, the narrator, knows that as well as anyone. White, female, 26, convicted of night time breaking and entering with force, she works in the prison law library, giving legal counsel of more-or-mostly-less usefulness to other convicts. More useful is the hootch stash she keeps behind the law books.

And she has plenty of enemies—like Johnson, the lesbian-hating warden, and Alex, the "pretty little dude" lawyer who doesn't like her free legal advice. Then there's Rosalie and Birdeye—serious rustlers whose loyalty lasts about as long as their cigarettes hold out. And then there's China: Latina, female, 22, holding US citizenship through marriage, convicted of conspiracy to commit murder—a dangerous woman who is safer in prison than she is on the streets. They're all trying to get through without getting caught or going straight, but there's just one catch—a bloodstained bank account that everybody wants, including some players on the outside. *Low Bite*: an underground classic reprinted at last and the first title in the new imprint from The Green Arcade.

"Vicious, funny, cunning, ruthless, explicit… a tough original look at inside loves and larcenies."
— Kirkus Reviews

"Where else can you find the grittiness of girls-behind-bars mixed with intelligence, brilliant prose, and emotional ferocity? Sin Soracco sets the standard for prison writing. Hardboiled and with brains!"
— Peter Maravelis, editor *San Francisco Noir* 1 and 2

"Tells a gripping story concerning a group of women in a California prison: their crimes, their relationships, their hopes and dreams."
— *Publisher's Weekly*

"Sin Soracco is the original Black Lizard. Low Bite *will take a chunk out of your leg if not your heart. Read it, it will devour you."*
— Barry Gifford, author *Port Tropique*, Founder Black Lizard Books

The Incredible Double

Owen Hill

ISBN: 978-1-60486-083-2

$13.95   144 pages

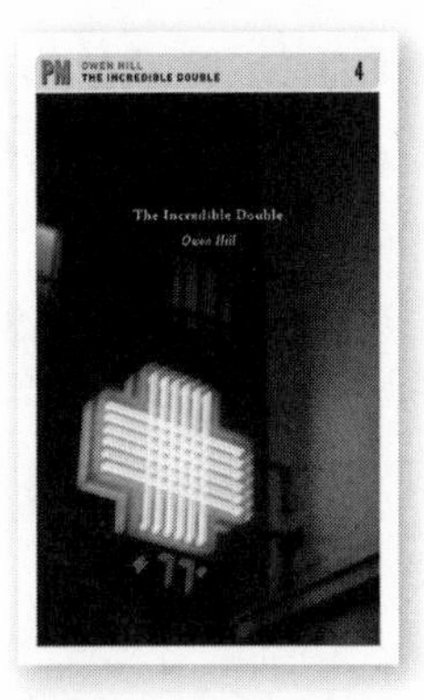

Clay Blackburn has two jobs. Most of the time he's your average bisexual book scout in Berkeley. Some of the time he's . . . not quite a private detective. He doesn't have a license, he doesn't have a gun, he doesn't have a business card—but people come to him for help and in helping them he comes across more than his fair share of trouble. And trouble finds him seeking the fountain of youth, the myth of paradise, the pie in the sky . . . The Incredible Double.

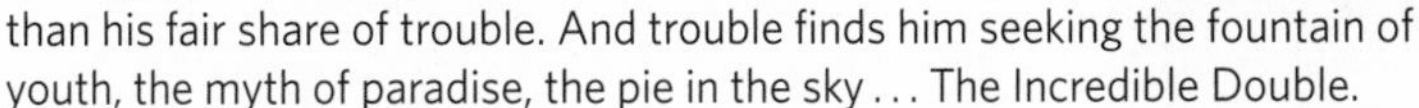

Clay fights his way through corporate shills, Berkeley loonies, and CEO thugs on his way to understanding the secret of The Double. Follow his journey to a state of Grace, epiphanies, perhaps the meaning of life. This follow-up to *The Chandler Apartments*, red meat to charter members of the Clay Blackburn cult, is also an excellent introduction to the series. Hill brings back Blackburn's trusty, if goofy sidekicks: Marvin, best friend and lefty soldier of fortune; Bailey Dao, ex-FBI agent; Dino Centro, as smarmy as he is debonair. He also introduces a new cast of bizarre characters: drug casualty turned poet Loose Bruce, conspiracy theorist Larry Sasway, and Grace, the Tallulah Bankhead of Berkeley. Together—and sometimes not so together—they team up to foil Drugstore Wally, the CEO with an evil plan.

"Very well written, well paced, well time-lined and well-charactered. I chuckled seeing so many of my poetic acquaintances mentioned in the text."
— Ed Sanders

"Owen Hill's breathless, sly and insouciant mystery novels are full of that rare Dawn Powell-ish essence: fictional gossip. I could imagine popping in and out of his sexy little Chandler building apartment a thousand times and never having the same cocktail buzz twice. Poets have all the fun, apparently."
— Jonathan Lethem author of *The Fortress of Solitude*

"Guillaume Appollinaire and Edward Sanders would feast on this thriller of the real Berkeley and its transsexual CIA agents and doppelgangers staging Glock shoot-outs. A mystery of contingencies centering in the reeking Chandler Arms and the quicksand of Moe's Books."
— Michael McClure

FOUND IN TRANSLATION from PM Press

Calling All Heroes: A Manual for Taking Power

Paco Ignacio Taibo II

ISBN: 978-1-60486-205-8
$12.00 128 pages

The euphoric idealism of grassroots reform and the tragic reality of revolutionary failure are at the center of this speculative novel that opens with a real historical event. On October 2, 1968, 10 days before the Summer Olympics in Mexico, the Mexican government responds to a student demonstration in Tlatelolco by firing into the crowd, killing more than 200 students and civilians and wounding hundreds more. The Tlatelolco massacre was erased from the official record as easily as authorities washing the blood from the streets, and no one was ever held accountable. It is two years later and Nestor, a journalist and participant in the fateful events, lies recovering in the hospital from a knife wound. His fevered imagination leads him in the collection of facts and memories of the movement and its assassination in the company of figures from his childhood. Nestor calls on the heroes of his youth—Sherlock Holmes, Doc Holliday, Wyatt Earp, and D'Artagnan among them—to join him in launching a new reform movement conceived by his intensely active imagination.

"Taibo's writing is witty, provocative, finely nuanced and well worth the challenge."
— *Publishers Weekly*

"I am his number one fan. . . I can always lose myself in one of his novels because of their intelligence and humor. My secret wish is to become one of the characters in his fiction, all of them drawn from the wit and wisdom of popular imagination. Yet make no mistake, Paco Taibo—sociologist and historian—is recovering the political history of Mexico to offer a vital, compelling vision of our reality."
— Laura Esquivel, author of *Like Water for Chocolate*

"The real enchantment of Mr. Taibo's storytelling lies in the wild and melancholy tangle of life he sees everywhere."
— *New York Times Book Review*

"It doesn't matter what happens. Taibo's novels constitute an absurdist manifesto. No matter how oppressive a government, no matter how strict the limitations of life, we all have our imaginations, our inventiveness, our ability to liven up lonely apartments with a couple of quacking ducks. If you don't have anything left, oppressors can't take anything away."
— *Washington Post Book World*